Please turn to the back
of the book for an interview with
Joyce Christmas.

Pete and Jack Thurlow found the body an hour or two later when the tide was fully out and the fog had settled in firmly on the beach and the cove. . . . The boys had almost turned back before they reached the cove, but Pete, the older one, had seen something that interested him. A pale pile of fabric in the tidal pool over which wisps of fog hung. It could be a life jacket or a sail, something rare and wonderful, a real treasure. That's when they found her. They looked at each other with momentary terror. A gentle prod with the trusty sneaker revealed her white face, wrinkled by submersion, but they didn't dare touch her. They stared, the eleven-year-old hoping that his year-older brother would know what to do.

"We better get Dad," Pete said. Then Jack spotted a round silver object between the rocks. That was a real treasure for sure. . . .

By Joyce Christmas
Published by Fawcett Books:

A Better Class of Murder

A Lady Margaret Priam/
Betty Trenka Mystery

Joyce Christmas

FAWCETT BOOKS · NEW YORK

A Fawcett Book
Published by The Ballantine Publishing Group
Copyright © 2000 by Joyce Christmas

www.randomhouse.com/BB/

Library of Congress Catalog Card Number: 00-107300

ISBN 0-449-15013-5

Manufactured in the United States of America

First Ballantine Books Edition: December 2000

10 9 8 7 6 5 4 3 2 1

This book honors my friends
Margery Flar and Dina Willner,
dedicated mystery readers.

CHAPTER 1

ALMOST NO one noticed the little green car creeping along the fog-shrouded roads of Redding's Point, a summer beach resort on Long Island Sound in Connecticut. There was almost no one to notice, since most of the summer people had departed and the few locals were barricaded in their winterized homes with shades drawn against the foggy night. Except for Stan Thurlow, who had abandoned his cozy living room and taken Venture, the household's clumsy black lab, for his evening walk.

Stan had Venture on a leash but was intending to let the dog run on the beach, something forbidden during the summer months, but as a year-round resident Stan felt that the beach was his and Venture's.

The car pulled into a stretch of grass above the beach while Stan and the dog were still a distance away, but he saw two people get out. The fog wrapped around them like shawls as they found the steps down to the sand. Maybe Stan wouldn't take the dog to the beach after all, lest he alarm them. He

1

couldn't tell what sex they were, but then he heard a woman's voice say, "It's weird. I love it." She took off her shoes so that she could dig her toes into the sand. It wasn't cold or even chilly. Stan approached the beach and watched as she danced along in the waves that broke gently on the land. The tide was going out, and she left a trail of footprints in the damp sand. Her dark hair floated behind her as she disappeared into the fog. Her companion appeared to be watching her, then followed. Stan was curious about them, because not too many casual visitors turned up at Redding's Point, but he continued on with the dog along a road away from the beach. Venture would have to have his run another night.

The two strollers finally came together where the beach ended in an outcropping of sea-smoothed boulders. The woman dropped her shoes in the sand and climbed up on a rock, signaling to the dark shape of her companion.

"Catch me if you can," she called, and her voice was taunting. The other clambered unsteadily onto the rock beside the woman, grasped her arm, and said, "Give me what's mine."

"Don't be so melodramatic. It's not yours." She laughed. "It's mine now anyhow." She took a silvery object from the pocket of her slacks and held it high in the air. "What a lovely idea coming here to the beach. It's magical."

"It's mine," the other said, and put a hand to the

woman's throat. She pulled away, but the other held on tightly and tried to reach for the silver object, to no avail. The woman struggled slightly, lost her footing, and crashed facedown into a tidal pool at the foot of the rocks. The other carefully slid down the rocks and pressed a foot on the woman's neck as she struggled to lift her face out of the water. After a long moment, her thrashing stopped and the silver object was no longer in her hand.

The other decided it must be at the bottom of the tidal pool but couldn't see it. Somewhere behind the fog and clouds there was a full moon, but no light penetrated the mist. The tide would probably take the silver object away as the water ebbed. It would be swept out to sea. In some ways, that would be for the best. Away at the other end of the beach, the headlights of a car crossed the causeway. The other carefully climbed back over the rocks and onto the beach, then returned to the green car, keeping close to the seawall, though the fog bestowed the gift of invisibility.

The little green car backed up to the road and moved away quietly. The lights weren't switched on until it had passed the row of summer cottages and turned onto the street that led from the beach colony back to the main road. The other car must have pulled into the driveway of one of the few houses with lights among the many that were dark and closed up for the season.

The dead woman had been pretty, a charming

friend. Desirable and witty. It was a pity to lose her, but business was business, and if she chose to play games, she had to suffer the consequences. There was a long drive ahead. No point in worrying about that business on the beach.

It rained during the night, and high tide came again very early in the morning, filling the tidal pool and rocking the floating body gently. No one ventured along the beach until midday, when a new bank of fog rolled in across the slick surface of Long Island Sound. It was dense and determined, soon hiding the two little offshore islands and reaching the gently sloping beach, where modest waves broke daintily on the wet sand. The fog crept up the narrow creek that had cut a path through the wetlands and emptied into the bay.

At the end of the beach, where a pile of water-smoothed boulders formed a rocky cove and the water stood a foot deep, clusters of blue-black mussels attached to the rocks floated their beards in the retreating tide and six tiny green crabs clambered across the pebbles, the empty shells, the bits of blue and brown sea glass. They skittered across the pale white hand that floated in the pool, became entangled in the long black hair that covered the surface, and scuttled around a silvery object wedged in a crevice between the rocks. But they didn't pause at the slim body that lay facedown in the water. The tide was rapidly retreating, and they went with the flow, out of the cove and into the deeper offshore water.

Pete and Jack Thurlow found the body an hour or two later when the tide was fully out and the fog had settled in firmly on the beach and the cove. The boys had been scouring the beach for sea-tossed treasures abandoned by the waves created by a meek autumn storm a few days earlier before the fog appeared yesterday: a piece of rope, an odd shell, a tangle of nylon fishing line with sinkers and hooks still attached. They had marveled at the very dead seagull with tattered feathers and had used the toe of a sneaker to flip over a stranded horseshoe crab. The survivor of primordial times and the dangers of modern weather had then inched its way back across the sand toward the safety of the water.

The summer was over, the summer people had gone back to their homes upstate. The boys remained because they were locals and lived with their family beside the Sound year-round in the now mostly deserted beach colony, with streets of boarded-up cottages and empty yards. They had to entertain themselves through the boring, quiet days of autumn and the oddly beautiful days of winter, when snow fell on the beach and was licked away along the edges by the rising tides. On the rare freezing-cold days, they found rims of ice had formed on the rocks around the cove and even the salty tidal pools would sometimes show a thin cover of ice.

The boys had almost turned back before they reached the cove, but Pete, the older one, had seen something that interested him. A pale pile of fabric in the tidal pool over which wisps of fog hung. It could be a life jacket or a sail, something rare and wonderful, a real treasure. That's when they found her. They looked at each other with momentary terror. A gentle prod with the trusty sneaker revealed her white face, wrinkled by submersion, but they didn't dare touch her. She certainly appeared to be dead. They stared, the eleven-year-old hoping that his year-older brother would know what to do.

"We better get Dad," Pete said. Then Jack spotted a round silver object between the rocks. That was a real treasure for sure. He pulled it out and put it in his pocket, not telling his brother, who in any case was examining a pair of women's shoes left on the sand. Then they ran back along the beach, up the stairs the summer people used to descend to the sand loaded down with beach towels and chairs, umbrellas and books, and sunscreen. But there was no one else on the beach now. The boys ran along the narrow roads and past empty, staring windows to their house, an old summer cottage that had been made over into a year-round home, snug and quiet in the midst of the deeper serenity of seasonal abandonment. Oh, there were a few people around in some of the other cottages, people who refused to admit that summer was over and chose to stay on in chilly, damp rooms just a few days longer. Could the dead woman be one of them? The boys hadn't recognized her as being one of the handful of other year-round residents.

Their father, Stan Thurlow, called the resident Connecticut state trooper in the nearby town and went back to the tidal pool with the boys to be sure that they were telling the truth. They were. The water had almost drained away, and the slim body lay on the sandy and pebbled bottom of the pool, face-down, her hair plastered to her back. Stan didn't recognize her either, but he realized that she was probably the woman he'd seen the night before. Whatever had happened, her companion had fled, leaving her there.

"She must have drowned," the father said. "We'll wait for the cops to tell us what really happened. You boys go on home now. I don't want you seeing this."

But of course they wanted to see all of it. It was the best thing that had ever happened to them in the off season, better than a dead gull, better than the hurricane that had lashed its way across the Sound last fall and briefly cut them off from the rest of the world when the road into Redding's Point had flooded. It was better even than the time the Fourth of July fireworks had gotten out of hand and a whole pile of them had gone off all at once.

The police came and questioned the boys.

"You kids didn't see any strangers around, did you? Any cars you didn't recognize?"

They'd seen no one on the beach, they'd touched nothing. Jack didn't mention the silver thing in his pocket. Indeed, he'd forgotten it in the gory excitement of seeing the body moved to a stretcher and taken away, and anyhow he wasn't overly concerned with crime scenes and evidence. Pete showed the policeman the shoes. Stan noticed that the young woman seemed to have been good-looking, not at all disfigured by her mishap, but perhaps those were bruises on her neck and arms. He noticed a ring on one finger with a hefty, pretty colored stone.

"I'll let ya know what happened, Stan, when we find out what killed her," the state policeman said. He'd known Stan for a good many years. They were pals. "She might have fallen off a boat out on the Sound during that storm. I'll check with the Coast Guard." He looked around at the all-encompassing fog that seemed to be getting heavier by the minute.

"I hate these damned foggy days. Accidents on the roads, kids up to mischief in town because they think nobody can see them. End of summer for sure. Wonder if she was one of the summer people. Didn't find any ID on her." He spoke sternly to Pete and Jack. "If you boys find anything on the beach like a handbag, be sure you get it to me pronto."

"Yessir," they said as one, and immediately set off to scavenge.

Stan knew he had to tell his friend what he'd seen. "I was walking our dog last night and noticed a car parked on the right-of-way just above the beach." He gestured toward the steps and the stretch of grass that gave people access to the beach. "Two people got out, but it was so foggy, I couldn't tell whether they were men or women or what kind of car it was. Then I heard a woman's voice. They went down to the beach and the dog and I continued on back home. Never thought another thing about it."

"Pretty rare to get visitors this time of year," the state policeman said. Stan agreed, but there was nothing more he could tell the cop. It had been too foggy and dark to notice the license plate on the car, although he thought it had been a light color.

"We're probably looking at a lovers' quarrel," the cop said. "Kind of an odd place to break up, as it were, don't you think? Unless the guy lived around here." Again Stan agreed and wondered if his friend the policeman was looking at him in an odd way.

"I didn't recognize her," Stan said. "And my wife and the boys will tell you I was out with the dog just a little while. And you know I don't fool around with women."

"I'm not suggesting anything," the policeman said. "The Major Crime boys will want to know. Too bad you didn't get a closer look at the pair and the car."

When the boys got home, Jack pulled Pete down to the basement, out of earshot of their parents, and displayed his find. Pete thought the silver thing his brother had found near the body was a computer disk. It certainly hadn't played music on his CD player, and he didn't own a computer, knew little about them.

"Dad's not going to like this," Pete said. "It's like . . . evidence or something." They'd watched enough cop shows on television to know that withholding evidence was not a good thing, so they decided to postpone any trouble they might be in and hid the disk in a drawer and tried to forget about it. But they both knew they'd end up confessing, eventually.

Meanwhile, word of the discovery of a body on the beach spread through the last of the summer people and into the nearby small town. The local paper picked it up and a photo of Pete and Jack Thurlow appeared on the front page. The local television news even had a story or two on the dead woman and showed an artist's sketch of her face.

It was a day or two later that investigators came across a sodden lump of leather in the tidal pool that turned out to be a wallet. It had probably belonged to the dead woman.

The police went about trying to locate someone who had known Jane Xaviera Corvo, identified by her California driver's license. She had died by drowning in a small tidal pool on the Connecticut coast just before a really big fog rolled in and covered much of the state and others nearby. According to reports, her death had probably been aided by some human intervention, because there were bruises on her neck. They seemed to indicate that she'd been murdered.

The tides ebbed and flowed while a fruitless search

for anyone who had known the dead woman continued on both coasts. Then the authorities located her mother near San Diego. Mrs. Corvo wept, but not for long.

"Janie went her own way, never called me, kept moving here, there, mostly in California, but then I think she moved east. I never knew where she was, who she was with. She liked money and she was really pretty, so she attracted men with money. We're not rich people. We weren't good enough for her. What did she do? She worked for a while at a company that had something to do with computers. I don't think she knew anything about them, she just worked in the office, but she got involved with the boss, an important guy, and rich, of course, so she started putting on airs. Even changed her name to something fancier than Jane. Her name was not Xaviera. She started calling herself that, but she was just Jane, that was the name I gave her. Jane. I hope you find the person who killed her."

"It may have been a terrible accident, Mrs. Corvo. She may have slipped overboard from some boat or on the wet rocks, hit her head and drowned in the tidal pool."

"Xaviera." Mrs. Corvo sniffed. "Will I have to put that name on her tombstone?"

CHAPTER 2

GRAY. EVERYTHING was gray. Elizabeth Trenka looked out the second-floor bedroom window of her little white house in East Moulton, Connecticut. An autumn fog had been lingering for at least two days, curling around the blue spruce in front of the house and hanging like a blanket across Timberhill Road. It hid Ted Kelso's low stone house across the road. It was a gray banner stretching from the low-lying clouds to the ground, signaling that the season had changed overnight. Summer had ended abruptly.

She felt as gray as the day. When she looked in the bathroom mirror, it seemed to her that her very face was drawn and gray and the thick brown hair that had remained unchanged for all of her sixty-plus years was now threaded with . . . gray.

She had awakened with a slight headache, which probably contributed to her feelings of gloom. She must have slept in a funny position and was feeling the effects of it on her aging body. Even Tina, her mildly dreadful cat, remained curled up at the foot of the bed as though she, too, was unwilling to face the day. Usually Tina was pleased to complain loudly that breakfast was wanted immediately.

Oppressed in mind and body, Betty went down to the living room and turned on the TV to check the news and weather. Neither sounded good.

There was another story about the woman who had been found dead on the beach downstate on the Sound. The phrases *mysterious* and *suspected foul play* were emphasized by the newscaster, who seemed to relish the sordid details, which were sketchy at best. Then Betty heard that the weather front that had moved across the state yesterday, bringing the fog, remained stationary. The gray wasn't going to go away until maybe late afternoon. It didn't matter much. She had no place to go to today. No office to drive to. That had ended with her enforced retirement a few years back, when Edwards & Son had shown her the door with little ceremony. She had no temporary work just now, although in the past she had been fortunate enough to find a few paying tasks in the little town she had moved to after retirement.

She wasn't a hobbyist, she didn't have a book she wanted to read, she wasn't about to take up baking after all her years of resisting every form of domestic arts. In any case the house was tidy, the laundry was done, and the few articles of clothing that needed ironing could wait until they were needed.

She glanced toward the dining room, where her computer resided. Her neighbor Ted Kelso had

finally convinced her to get on the Internet and make
E-mail friends. Ted knew all about computers and
had taught her a lot of things besides the word pro-
cessing and spreadsheets she'd done when she was
working. She was learning to enjoy surfing the Internet, but she hadn't started any electronic conversations to speak of. She didn't have a lot of friends, and
most of them were getting on in years. Sixty-year-old
women like her and her friends were not inclined
to swan-dive into the information age with gay
abandon. The electronic world had mostly passed
them by.

Once in a while Ted sent her a message from
across the street, and she'd briefly stepped into a couple of chat rooms but found the messages flying back
and forth too confusing to follow. Anyhow, she had
detected erotically charged subtexts in some of the
exchanges and felt she was a bit too old for that kind
of business. Still, she'd found that exploring the Internet was frequently entertaining—all those Web
sites crammed with fascinating bits of information,
the links to distant corners of the world. She might
take a look at some new sites a bit later.

After making herself coffee and feeding Tina, who
had suddenly decided that any dish of food was
worth considering, Betty dragged herself back up-
stairs to dress. Naturally she chose a thick gray
sweatshirt and corduroy slacks to match her mood
and the day. She could hear the television news from

downstairs, a collection of stories that did nothing to cheer her: fires, murders, a politician caught in a juicy scandal. Will they never learn? she wondered. The dead woman again. Probable foul play mentioned again. What was the world coming to?

Then she thought that there must be places that were sunny and full of color, with interesting sights and people, and right then she decided that she'd spend the morning looking at the guidebooks to exotic places she'd been collecting for years. She now had enough money to take the trips she'd always dreamed of. Sid Edwards Senior had ensured that she would be comfortable financially for the rest of her life, even if Sid Junior couldn't wait to see the last of her, or his father either, who had been removed from the company as unceremoniously as she. As office manager at Edwards & Son, she had always felt connected to the world because she had had a job she enjoyed, had worked with people she liked. She still missed that purposeful, organized business life that she'd lived for thirty-five years. She hadn't yet found another pattern of living that would sustain her for the next couple of decades. It might have been the oppressive fog, but she was feeling especially useless this morning.

At least her headache was fading, but everything was still gray. Even black-and-white Tina disappeared completely into the mist when Betty let her out for her morning stalk. The one car that passed her house was nearly invisible except for its dim headlights cutting through the fog as it sped along Timberhill Road.

With a sigh, Betty pulled down a handful of books about foreign countries from the bookshelf. Here was one about the Czech Republic, from which her family had emigrated a generation ago, back when it was still part of the Austro-Hungarian Empire. Prague and Vienna—those were places to dream about. London—she'd like to see London. And Italy—olive trees and Renaissance churches, cappuccino and espresso, Mount Vesuvius and Naples, Rome and the Forum. A bit of wanderlust stirred in her. She would definitely start planning a trip for the spring. The passport she'd gotten some months before—her very first—was safely tucked away in a drawer in the desk on which her computer rested. But the approach of autumn and then winter made spring seem far away. Her mood reverted to gray.

"Elizabeth Anne," she said out loud, "pull yourself together." Betty preferred to think of herself as Elizabeth, although few others cared to address her that way. To almost everybody she was just Betty. Well, she'd had plenty of time to get used to it.

The morning passed slowly as she read a guidebook about London. Westminster Abbey, the Tate Gallery, Trafalgar Square, the British Museum, Kew Gardens. Now and then she glanced out the window to find that the fog seemed to be getting thicker and grayer as the minutes passed. She might have driven to East Moulton center or out to the mall on the highway, just for something to do, but she didn't care to be on the road in such dangerous conditions. She could always walk across the field to visit with Penny Saks, her cheery young neighbor. The four boys—three blond ones, all called Whitey, and Penny's nephew, Tommy—would be at school, so the house would be quiet, but on a day like this Penny would certainly be plunged into one of her complicated crafts projects and would try to persuade Betty to participate.

No macramé for this old dame, Betty thought. And no knitting lessons or stenciling either. She opened a book about Italy and glimpsed a photo of a steep flight of steps rising up between ancient brick buildings with orange tile roofs and a bell tower in the distance against a blue, blue sky. No gray cloud of fog settled on the ground there. Even the photos of London—the Houses of Parliament, Big Ben, and Piccadilly Circus—showed cloudless skies, although Betty remembered hearing about great London fogs in years past. She imagined Jack the Ripper and Sherlock Holmes making their way through foggy London streets, the one to murder, the other to solve a crime.

Finally she went to her computer and turned it on. Lines of meaningless white text appeared on the black screen, indicating that it was warming itself up for her pleasure. Then a blue screen with neat rows of icons looked at her blankly. She connected to the

Internet to see if she had any E-mail messages, although it seemed unlikely that she would.

Aha! She had mail! Alas, one message was spam promoting online gambling. She didn't think so and deleted it. Another seemed to be a gateway to a teen pornography site. She deleted it without even looking further. The last message carried Ted Kelso's familiar E-mail address; this one she did open and read.

```
Elizabeth, I have a
business proposition if
you're interested. Come
across around eleven and
we'll talk about it. Ted.
```

Of course she was interested. Ted knew that she picked up work whenever it presented itself—as an office temp, a typist, even a temporary school secretary. She couldn't bear to be idle, even though she wasn't really good at thinking of things to do on her own. She needed an assignment, a purpose. She wondered what business Ted could possibly have that involved her.

Since he was largely confined to a wheelchair, he seldom went out to conduct business but worked at something from his home. She had only a vague idea of what he actually did do, although he was often busy with tasks of some kind, and she knew he was paid for doing them.

They had never really discussed either his condition or his profession, but she thought he did something with computers and he'd once mentioned testing software, whatever that meant.

Perhaps now that she was becoming more adept at finding things on the Internet, he wanted her to do some research for him. That might be fun, although he could just as easily do it himself. He spent most of his time at his computer. She didn't want to do chores for him simply because he felt sorry for her lack of occupation. Nor would he care to think she felt sorry for him. Although bound to a wheelchair, he refused to admit that there were things he simply could not do, so he did everything from cooking to keeping his house in order, gardening and maintaining a few hives of bees. He said bees were interesting, although Betty hadn't yet grasped their appeal. He even took a few carefully arranged trips, and of course he had a car fitted out for him to drive easily. She sometimes felt ashamed that she was not as self-sufficient and interested in things as Ted, and if he had dreamed up a task for her, even out of charity, she should accept it gracefully. Doing something was better than doing nothing.

She'd worry about that later. So she sent him a reply to his E-mail:

```
I'll be there, if I can
find my way through the
fog. Elizabeth.
```

Eleven was still more than two hours away. She summoned up a couple of travel sites on the Internet, but none of them did much more than mention well-known sights and list hotels and restaurants and the like. She'd have to look further. So she spent the rest of the time until she was due at Ted's house looking at screens of hotels, airline schedules, and weather forecasts around the world. Then she went back to her books, wondering again if she was really too old for all this electronic business, so empty of real human contact. Even the chat rooms she'd visited were impersonal, merely words that popped up on the screen, even when the words were expressing deep feelings like loneliness or fear or joy. Books were heavy and real. She liked the feel of them in her hands.

By the time she had to leave to visit Ted Kelso, she saw that the fog was beginning to thin and a weak sun was attempting to break through the woolly mist. She could clearly see the outlines of the tall pines behind Ted's house. The Weather Channel suggested that the skies would definitely be clear by the afternoon and the fog that had been blanketing the entire East Coast for days would finally depart, although it would perhaps return briefly on the morrow as the weather fronts with their warm and colder airs set up conditions for further airport chaos from Philadelphia and New York to Providence and Boston.

Fog was boring, she decided, and indeed, if Ted

had thought of something she could do, she'd jump at it. Boredom was something she refused to succumb to. She thought it was a sign of a terribly lazy mind. She filled Tina's food dish with some dry cat chow, which would greatly displease the little beast, and opened the kitchen door to let her in. Tina strolled heftily through the damp grass, where little pockets of fog still lay close to the ground. She noticed that Tina had apparently murdered a field mouse during her morning's adventures and was intending to present it to Betty.

"I don't want it," Betty said. "Don't try to get on my good side by bringing me a treat."

Tina dropped the mouse when Betty clapped her hands sharply. The cat streaked into the kitchen, where she sat glowering at the dry food, as if to say, "Where's the tuna?"

"I'll be back," Betty said. Tina didn't understand, and if she did, she wouldn't care to know what Betty was saying. Not for the first time Betty reminded herself to cease talking to Tina as if she were a human being.

She didn't bother to change her sweatshirt and slacks. Ted certainly didn't care how she was dressed. It was warm enough not to need a jacket, and her sneakers could handle the dampness underfoot.

The mail truck pulled up as she reached Timberhill Road.

"Morning, Miz Trenka," said old Mr. Spencer, the mailman, as he handed her a few pieces of mail that looked to be bills and flyers, although she did notice an envelope addressed in the properly nunnish hand of her cousin Sister Rita, now living in Boston.

"Good morning, Mr. Spencer. Strange weather we're having."

"Never saw a week like it. First that rain and now the fog. Heard the fog caused a couple of bad pileups on the highway yesterday and this morning. Nearly got smashed into myself while driving my route. Some idiot wasn't paying attention. You have a good day now." The mail truck pulled away and disappeared into the fog that still blanketed the road.

She was depressed by the lack of human contact in her life, by the banal exchange of superficialities with a motorized mail carrier, by the purposelessness of her life at the moment. Retirement was supposed to have some good aspects, but she hadn't yet found them. She'd kept herself busy until now with temporary jobs and a few jolting events that needed her attention. It had sometimes been almost exciting, even if a fair number of people had ended up dead. She wouldn't wish for that again, but still, it had all made her feel useful.

She crossed the road carefully, mindful of Mr. Spencer's brush with the idiot driver, and walked up the path to Ted's door. The lights were on inside the house. She rang the bell, waited a moment, then let herself in, calling Ted's name as she entered. She hated to make him come to the door, even though the polished wood floors made moving his wheelchair easy. But if he were not in his chair, he'd have to get into it or find his crutches and somehow make his way to her, and she didn't like to cost him that extra effort.

"Well, Elizabeth. On time as usual." Ted was sitting at his computer, typing something on the keyboard. Black letters on a white background. He saved his work and the screen went gray, but he didn't turn off the computer. "Have a seat. I'll be right with you after I make us some coffee."

Betty sat and opened her letter from Sister Rita. They exchanged a letter a month, just to keep in touch. Rita's letters usually detailed the little happenings at the homeless women's shelter that her order maintained in a run-down section of Boston, comments on the women she met, the adventures of the other sisters. Betty's letters were generally boring nowadays when she had no lively office events to report in the way she'd had for more than thirty years.

She thought about that. She and Rita had been corresponding for more than three decades, ever since Rita had professed her vows and later gone out to work in the world. In the beginning, Betty had been an inexperienced but eager young woman starting her job for Sid Edwards Senior at his small manufacturing company near Hartford. She'd gotten her own place in Hartford so that she wouldn't have to commute between the family home and her job.

Her parents, especially Pop, hadn't liked the idea of her taking a job away from the small Connecticut town where they lived, but eventually it became clear to them that their Elizabeth wasn't going to attract a suitable husband and become a housewife. "She's too damned plain, and taller than most fellows," she'd overheard Pop telling Ma. "She might as well be out earning money." So she'd devoted herself to Edwards & Son, growing more capable in her work and closer to Sid. Soon enough, they knew the bond between them was more than boss and employee. It was love, but in those more innocent times, it pretty much stopped there with the emotion and Betty's total devotion to him, which had not wavered through all the years. Even now, as he lay motionless in a nursing home suffering the aftereffects of a stroke, not a day passed that she didn't think of him or a week when she didn't visit his bedside. All too soon, she knew, his feeble grasp on life would weaken and he would be gone from her life.

Rita had been about the only person in whom she had truly confided anything about Sid and their growing attachment. All Rita had ever said was to remember that he was a married man and not to find herself sinning. After that, Rita had said no more on the subject and had let Betty ramble on for decades about Sid Edwards and Edwards & Son without comment or condemnation.

She quickly scanned Rita's letter to the end. Nothing startling. Old Minnie, one of the women the sisters looked after, had finally stopped drinking. A baby had been born in the shelter to a woman who had fled her abusive husband. Sister Maureen was studying for yet another advanced degree.

The usual news, except for a short postscript after "Love and prayers, Rita." It said, "We are both living in our sunset years, dear Elizabeth, and by the grace of God, I believe that I have accomplished much of what I set out to do. I wonder if you feel the same way, or if you have denied yourself that sense of true accomplishment. You should seize the years left to you and meet new challenges. You would be welcome here to work with the sisters among the unfortunate women we harbor, but whatever arises along your path, I urge you to accept the tasks that will be offered to you."

Suddenly, she wanted to see Rita. They seldom had a chance to visit, so it had been years since they'd come face-to-face, but she was Betty's only living relative. Just as Ted wheeled over to the sofa where she was sitting, she decided that whatever Ted wanted her to do she would accept it. Rita seemed to understand that something was about to be offered that would be important. When that was done, she'd drive up to Boston for a weekend and talk to Rita about her life and what she should do with it.

"Elizabeth, you're looking well on this gray day," Ted said. He handed her a mug of coffee.

"They say the fog will burn off by afternoon, and then we'll have a nice autumn day for a change."

"Followed by a heavy winter, I'm afraid. I'm a great believer in the message of the woolly caterpillars, and they seem ready for a hard season ahead. I've found someone to replace Brad Melville to get the hives in shape for winter. Someone with a better character at least, and Tommy has been pitching in to help. He seems quite happy and stable nowadays living with his aunt Penny and the boys."

"Yes, he's fine," Betty said, and glanced down again at Rita's letter. "You wanted me to do something for you?"

Ted looked up at the ceiling, over at his bookcases, the computer with the stacks of books and documents around it. Anywhere but at Betty, and she noticed his hesitation.

"Don't be coy, Ted. As long as it doesn't have anything to do with murder, I'll do it."

He laughed uneasily. "No murders, at least not that I know of. But speaking of murder, did you hear the report about the dead woman down at the shore? It's a small world thing. I know the place. My parents used to rent a house there almost every summer when I was growing up. I imagine it hasn't changed much in all these years, except to get more built up. We used to have a baseball diamond where we'd play every night until it got too dark to see the ball, and my father and his cronies even built a little nine-hole golf course for themselves. I suppose land near the ocean is too valuable to waste on games, so they've probably put up modern summer cottages instead of the old brown-shingled houses I remember. Wonder what became of the kids I used to hang out with.

They're probably all old fogies like me now." Ted wasn't old at all, just somewhere in his forties. In spite of his lack of mobility, he kept himself in good shape, and he was, Betty thought, an attractive-looking man. She tried to imagine Ted as a boy running the bases and catching fly balls in the outfield. At least he hadn't been disabled all his life.

"About the thing I'd like you to do for me, Elizabeth," he said. "I wonder if you'd be willing to uproot yourself for a few days and take a little trip as a favor to me. It's business."

"Does it require new clothes?"

"Ah, yes. 'Beware of enterprises that require a new wardrobe.' I think anything you have left over from your working days will suit. I merely want you to go to New York to interview a man who wants me to do some work for him. I'd do it myself, but it's not that easy to get around in the city in a wheelchair, and I don't yet feel secure on the crutches. Besides, I trust your judgment about people, even better than I trust my own. He's involved in computer software, and you may remember that one of my occupations is testing software."

"Ted, I know so little about that sort of stuff. Software and hardware. It's all a mystery to me."

"I don't want you to analyze his business. I want you to analyze *him*, get to know him, find out what he's like. It's all arranged if you agree. I'll put you up in a lovely hotel, provide an introduction to him and some nice people in the city, so you won't be totally on your own. You could go to the theater, visit some sights, and be wined and dined by the upper crust."

"In that event, I will definitely need a new wardrobe," Betty said. "Wining and dining outfits are few and far between in my closet. But of course I will do whatever you ask."

"Gerald Toth is a very rich man," Ted said. "You may have read about him. He is a West Coast type, right there in the middle of all that computer activity in Silicon Valley, but he happens to be in New York just now. He's not an innovator himself, but he certainly hires the best people to innovate for him, and he knows how to market the products his research and development people create. He knows, in short, how to make a lot of money."

"When do you want me to go? And you will tell me more, won't you?"

"Yes, you will hear all I know. How about within the next week? Say, on Monday. That will give me enough time to make the arrangements, but does it give you enough time to plan a Manhattan wardrobe?"

"If Penny will look after that damned cat, I can arrange it. There's nothing pending for me except to read guidebooks about places I might like to visit in the spring."

"It's time you got yourself out of East Moulton and saw the world," Ted said. "Travel can be a lot of fun. But business first. Come on over to the computer and I'll give you the background."

CHAPTER 3

"WE'VE NEVER really talked much about what I do," Ted said as he settled himself in front of his computer and tapped on a few keys. "I probably thought you wouldn't understand it, and I didn't want to bore you." After a moment the screen glowed blue with an array of icons. "You know I write a few articles for business publications, and I've even tried my hand at fiction, but with very little success." He grinned sheepishly. "I suppose everybody who lives with disability thinks he has something profound and moving to share."

"Every life has a story?" Betty was never comfortable talking about Ted's disability, and indeed never brought it up herself, although she listened thoughtfully whenever he chose to talk about it.

"Something like that," he said. "I make an effort not to miss out on too much. There's so much more I'd like to accomplish, but"—he nodded his head in the direction of his wheelchair—"there are barriers to meeting challenges." An echo of Sister Rita's letter again. Then he said, more brightly, "Therapy has helped with my crutches, so I don't have to career around the house in the wheelchair, and pretty soon I'll feel secure about venturing outside with them, right up to your front door. It'll be your turn to cook me dinner for a change."

"Ah, Ted, I wouldn't dream of competing with you in that department. Although I do make a pretty good Czech bean soup with dropped noodles. My mother taught me when I was a girl. Pop used to love it. It's about the only thing I can cook well from scratch."

"It's a deal then. Now about this job I have for you."

"And what you do."

"Me? Not to get too technical, but certain companies pay me good money to test new software programs before they release them to the public. Their programmers believe they've covered all the angles, have everything right, but somebody with no vested interest in simply confirming that belief has to see whether everything works the way it's supposed to. Sometimes they ask me to look at the programming code. I used to do some programming myself in the early days of computers. Anyhow, I can do my work at home, and it sure pays better than writing stories."

"I'd like to read one someday," Betty said, but Ted quickly brushed away the suggestion and went on with the task at hand.

"Gerald Toth thinks his people have developed the

greatest thing since sliced bread. An old friend from a different life, Ben Hoopes, recommended me to him, so Toth seems to think I'm the answer to his prayers. I can't go into details, but I doubt you'd care to hear them even if they weren't highly confidential." He paused. "There may be one small problem. Betty, are you listening?"

"What? Oh, yes, certainly. I'm sorry if I seemed inattentive. I was just wondering what the greatest thing before sliced bread was. Probably the wheel."

"Toth wants me to look at his software, give my opinion, check it out for him."

"But why would you need me to check out Mr. Toth? If you've worked in this business for a while, there must be others who know him that you could turn to for an opinion."

"The question of vested interests again. Or those others might not be truly objective. There could be quite a bit of money involved for me or whoever does the testing, and that's part of what's worrying me. He's willing to pay me far too much just to find the bugs and see that they're corrected before release. So I'm wondering if it's sort of a bribe to get me to say the right things. I'm a little uneasy about him. I'd like your opinion on whether he's to be trusted. Rumors have been floating around that Toth is in possession of a program developed by another company. I don't think he stole it personally, that's not his style. But maybe one of his people somehow pirated this new program and handed it over to Toth. Probably for a lot of money. I don't know him well enough to say whether he's dishonest, or willing to condone piracy, or anything else. Of course, people spread evil gossip on the Internet like they were scattering confetti on New Year's Eve. Some of it sticks, some of it gets swept into the gutter, but it doesn't go away."

Betty said, "It's not wise to get involved with a crime."

"The hottest rumor is that the software was developed by one of Toth's biggest competitors, Ivor Enterprises," Ted said. "Now Ivor Beame himself is a tough old character, he's been around this business for ages, and I wouldn't want to be on his bad side. I certainly don't want to be a party to criminal activity. Well, will you do the job for me?"

"But I really don't know a thing about computers, Ted, other than what you've taught me. I couldn't tell you anything about programming or software, and your Mr. Toth would know that immediately."

"But you *can* tell me something about people." Ted tapped a few keys on the keyboard and after a moment was connected to the Internet. He then typed in a URL and an elaborate page of pictures and text appeared on the screen. Betty leaned over his shoulder to look at it.

"Xaviera Corporation" read the banner across the top of the home page. Below it was a row of buttons. Ted clicked on one and a picture of a strikingly handsome man gradually appeared.

"That's your quarry," Ted said. "Gerald Toth. I'm

sure a downloaded Internet picture doesn't do him justice. Women have told me that he has the bluest eyes they've ever seen and they melt when he smiles. You'd better be prepared for him."

"Melt?" Betty said thoughtfully. "I don't think melting is part of my natural reaction to the opposite sex. Not that I don't admire a good-looking man, even at my age," she added hastily.

"I'm sure Toth has gotten a lot of mileage out of being a handsome lad," Ted said. "I keep reading about him in the gossip columns, he's quite the ladies' man. He's seen here and there with one beauty or another. Well, he can afford to treat them very well. If you'd like, I can print out the background on Xaviera Corporation so you'll know what his business is all about. He only started the company a few years ago, but he has done remarkably well with it."

"I suppose I should be fully prepared," Betty said. "Especially if he expects me to make pleasant conversation about his company."

"You probably know more than you think. You worked for Zig-Zag when you first moved to East Moulton, didn't you? They did software."

"Don't forget, Ted, I was merely a temp at Zig-Zag. I found a murderer, and I played tag with Mr. Mitsui, who was buying out the company. I had nothing to do with the computers except to turn one on to help the accounts receivable girl with the billing. Exactly what is it you want me to ask Mr. Toth?"

"I'll give you some suggestions, but I'll leave most of it to you, Elizabeth. I want to get a sense of what you feel about him. You must have had to size up some characters in your years in business."

"Oh, I did. Sid used to ask me to interview prospective employees on all levels. Of course, I mostly handled the office staff, but he would have me talk to people who might be coming on board in executive or sales positions. I never went far wrong. I remember one fellow who was applying for the director of sales job. He had a splendid résumé, talked a good game, but the eyes were all wrong."

"Eyes?"

"He wouldn't look me in the eye. Not once. I thought that was odd, because his résumé listed a lot of sales work, and I thought that certainly a skilled salesman would use eye contact to its full advantage. Now if I'd been some kind of femme fatale type, I could imagine that my exotic beauty might have been too distracting for him to look at me, but I definitely wasn't a raving beauty, able to turn men into so much quivering jelly, so I just asked him a few more questions about his previous jobs. That's when he got flustered and I knew I'd hit on something. It turned out that his résumé was a total fabrication. That might have been excused, a bit anyhow, because people always have résumés that make them sound better than they really are, but we made it a point to check some references and found out that he was pretty much a failure and previous employers even considered him to be a minor crook. I always wondered why he bothered to include them as references. We didn't hire him, of course."

"Because you noticed a lack of eye contact. You see? I knew I picked the right person for my job. Someone who's up to the challenge of seeing through Gerald Toth."

"Mr. Toth won't know why I'm talking to him, will he?"

Ted frowned. "Not exactly, but maybe a little. I couldn't figure out a way to get you two together without suggesting that you were a trusted lieutenant of mine. But don't worry. I'll give you some precise business-type questions to ask so he'll get the idea that you're just looking for background on the job he wants me to do, not background on the man himself."

Betty pondered what she was being asked to do. Then she felt a tiny thrill of anticipation about visiting New York. Of course she'd been there any number of times over the past few decades. It was easy back then to take a New York, New Haven and Hartford Railroad train from Hartford to New Haven, and then on to Manhattan, detraining at Grand Central Station. She missed the beautiful old Pennsylvania Station, so sadly razed years ago. Even the old rail company was gone, replaced by Amtrak.

She remembered the excitement of seeing her first Broadway musical, her first trip to the Metropolitan Museum of Art, the long hours spent in the Museum of Natural History, her first sight of the new United Nations building on First Avenue, and even the massive crowds on Fifth Avenue, more interesting to her than all the fashionable shops. How she'd like to do all that one more time, and now Ted was giving her the chance.

"How long do you suppose I'll be away?" she asked. "I mean, it can't be going to take me long to have a conversation with Mr. Toth."

"Plan on a week," Ted said. "I want you to proceed slowly enough so that he doesn't get the idea that you're some kind of dogged private investigator."

"Although I am," Betty said.

"I'd rather he thought of you as a tourist who just happens to be fitting in a bit of information-gathering for me."

"All right," she said. "A week. Nothing much to keep me in East Moulton, is there? I'll cancel my Wednesday volunteer stint at the library and talk to Penny this evening about looking after the cat. One of her boys can run over in the morning and at night to satisfy the beast's hunger. Then I'll get on to the question of what to wear, what I need to take. I suppose I'll drive down to New Haven to catch the train and leave my car in a parking lot or garage for the duration."

"Or I could drive you to New Haven to catch the Metro-North train and pick you up when you return." Ted's car was well equipped to handle his lack of mobility. He often said that the ability to drive about was the one thing that made him feel he wasn't a prisoner of his disability.

"If you're sure it wouldn't be too much trouble . . ."

"Elizabeth, you're doing me a favor, it's the least I can do for you. Now, if you travel on Monday and return the following Sunday, you should have enough time to see the sights and talk to Toth. I'll book you into a lovely little boutique hotel on the East Side called the Villa d'Este. It's owned by a woman named Carolyn Sue Hoopes, whose husband Ben Hoopes is the man who recommended me to Toth and is also a business acquaintance of mine. I'll call Carolyn Sue to say that you're coming, and if you're lucky, she may be in the city, although she lives most of the time in Dallas. I wonder what you'll make of her. She's very rich, indeed, and she used to be a princess, courtesy of a former marriage to a titled Italian."

"Rather rich for my blood," Betty said. "Remember, I come from a distinguished family of Czechoslovakian peasants, not from the upper classes at all. It certainly doesn't matter to me, but the rich seem to be highly conscious of class." But she was secretly charmed by the idea of meeting a princess.

Ted printed out the Web pages about Gerald Toth's Xaviera Corporation, including his color picture. Betty examined it. "He is rather strikingly attractive, isn't he," she said, "but 'Xaviera' doesn't sound much like a high-tech company."

Ted laughed. "Rumors abound about the name. Some say Xaviera was a Tijuana lady of the night who captured his fancy. Others say she was a Spanish noblewoman who caught his eye and then spurned him when he was a struggling entrepreneur with no money. So he was determined to make a pile of money and that would perhaps make him more desirable, especially if he went so far as to name his company after her. The most likely story is that she was just some pretty woman he fell in love with and lost. That must be hard on a man people say is irresistible. Especially if he believes his own press." Now Ted shut down his computer.

"Well, he's made the money, but I've never heard of any permanent woman in his life. He and his company are often mentioned in the *Wall Street Journal* and the *Financial Times,* and in just about every other business publication. I think he just wanted a company name that began with an X. Xerox was already taken, so he ended up with Xaviera. Maybe asking him about the name would be a conversational icebreaker."

Betty frowned.

"I can see you don't think much of the idea."

"I wonder if such a personal question would be appropriate."

"Right as usual, Elizabeth." Ted thought for a minute. "You could do an Internet search to find out where he's been written up by the press and what's been said about him. You know how to do that, don't you?"

"Certainly," Betty said. "I do it all the time for my own amusement when some subject interests me. And I even have a few regular E-mail correspondents. One of my old friends in Hartford isn't afraid of computers." She thought it would be nice if Sister Rita's community had E-mail so that Betty could be in closer touch with her cousin.

"I accept your offer, Ted, and now I really ought to be getting home and make myself some lunch. It looks as if the fog has almost lifted, so I can drive up to the mall on the highway or just into East Moulton and check out wining and dining clothes, if you really think that sort of thing will be on my agenda."

"Gerald Toth enjoys the finer things in life, so I'm sure he'll want to take you out to some nice places. And if the former Principessa Castrocani is in the city, you'll surely want to look your elegant best to impress her and her friends. Very social, Carolyn Sue is."

Betty chuckled to herself. She was quite tall for a woman and had never been accused of being a beauty and never thought of herself as elegant, not with her thick mop of hair and her heavy glasses. She was, in fact, too old to attempt elegance, and she was definitely not accustomed to mingling with very social people.

"I won't have to do myself up with all kinds of makeup, will I?"

"I'm sure if you put yourself together in a way that you're comfortable with, you'll do just fine, Elizabeth. And I can give you lunch here, if you'd like."

"Not today, Ted. You feed me far too often. Besides, I have a lot to do." She was actually looking forward to preparing for her trip to New York and was eager to get on with the organizing.

"Then we'll get together later in the week for a planning session, after you've read up on Toth and his company. I know you want to be prepared for anything, although it's going to be just a routine task. But I do thank you for taking it on. And if Penny and her boys can't handle that cat of yours, you can bring her over here and I'll see that she gets her grub."

That was generous of him. He didn't much like poor Tina either.

CHAPTER 4

THE FOG that engulfed the state of Connecticut was also swirling around the towers of Manhattan and surrounding territory, successfully bringing at least three major airports to a standstill and disconcerting those city inhabitants who bothered to notice that familiar landmarks like the towers of the World Trade Center and the Chrysler Building had disappeared from view.

Lady Margaret Priam, for one, drew the drapes in her East Side high-rise apartment, just to remove the sensation of being suspended in a cloud. She had no plans for the day except to sloth about and perhaps watch daytime television. She had once had a job working for an antiques dealer and later for a famed interior designer, but she was unemployed at the moment. She certainly didn't want to go out and aimlessly roam the murky streets of New York, looking at clothes she couldn't afford to buy. She really needed to find a job because her modest inheritance from her parents wouldn't last forever. That thought reminded her of her wonderfully efficient mother, the Countess of Brayfield, who had run the family estate of Priam's Priory and her children's lives with a firm hand.

The fog was still hanging there outside her high-rise building. She remembered another foggy day, this one a pea souper years before in London, when she and her mother had traveled down by train from Priam's Priory to shop at Harrods in Knightsbridge before she went off to finishing school in Switzerland. The day had ended with a lavish tea at Brown's Hotel. But feeling their way through a nearly invisible London had been terrifying. They had been lost until a kind bobby had loomed up in the fog and set them right. Ever since, though, she had disliked being outside on foggy days, not that there had been anything like a London fog in the decade she'd been living in New York.

Ah! The phone. Nice to know there was someone alive out there, although it was probably just another poor soul trapped at home by the weather.

"Margaret, honey, Ah've got the most tiresome business to take care of." How like Carolyn Sue Hoopes to plunge into a conversation and assume that everyone recognized her voice, her (possibly exaggerated) Texas drawl, her need to call upon friends to assist her in tiresome business.

"Carolyn Sue, where are you?"

"Right here in good old New York, darlin'. At the

Villa d'Este. Ah jus' got in, but Ah'm not stayin' long. This weather is purely hateful. Anyhow, my boy has his place full of houseguests. No room for his old momma." Carolyn Sue's son, Prince Paul, via the long-departed Prince Aldo Castrocani, inhabited an apartment in a Chelsea building owned by his mother, but since Carolyn Sue was also the owner of the charming and luxurious Villa d'Este hotel, she never lacked a place to rest her resolutely blond head. "Truth to tell, I'm more comfortable here at the hotel. Never did like washin' up the wares and runnin' the vacuum cleaner. I have people to do that for me back home in Dallas." Margaret knew that Carolyn Sue commanded an army of servants at her vast home in Texas; she had one woman whose sole responsibility was to look after the designer frocks in her wardrobe, which incidentally filled an entire room, and to be sure that Carolyn Sue's legendary jewel collection was kept polished and ready to be worn in an instant.

"I'm goin' to persuade Paul to hire a cleanin' lady to come in to do the chores I hate," she said. It seemed likely that Carolyn Sue had never done a chore in her life, since she'd been born rich and managed to retain that wealth in spite of marrying into impecunious nobility.

"I'm not sure De Vere would care for a cleaning lady," Margaret said. Margaret's on-again/off-again beau, Sam De Vere of the New York City police, shared the Chelsea apartment with Paul. "He keeps his gun around, and he doesn't like strangers in the place."

"I can handle Sam," Carolyn Sue said. "I'm sure he'd be right grateful to have the place kept neat and tidy."

"What's this tiresome business you mentioned?" Margaret liked to chat with Carolyn Sue, but just now the housekeeping details of Paul's apartment didn't interest her.

"One of Ben's business associates called me to say he's sending some kind of assistant to New York on business. She's going to be staying here at the d'Este, and he wants me to show her around, introduce her to some nice people, and I jus' don't have the time. I'm headin' out of town day after tomorrow for a nice revivin' week or two at a spa out in sunny Arizona. I want to get myself in shape for the winter holidays. You know how these women talk if you let yourself go just the tiniest bit."

Margaret didn't wait for her to ask if she, Margaret, would take over the entertaining duties. "I'll be glad to show the young lady around," she said, and hoped she would be nothing like the last young lady Carolyn Sue had shoved off on her. Precious little Lucy had been something of a chore, but that was partly because she'd stayed in Margaret's small guest bedroom, which was scarcely big enough for a bed, let alone Lucy's extensive wardrobe. There had to be something about wealthy Texas females and their clothes. . . .

"Well, honey, there seems to be a few complications."

Margaret waited.

"First of all, she's not a young lady. In fact, if I understand correctly, she's quite an old lady, retired from business. Lives up in Connecticut."

Margaret felt a sense of relief. Surely a retired old lady wouldn't expect too much in the way of bright lights and wild entertainment, unlike little Lucy, who could barely tear herself away from the hot downtown clubs of Manhattan. "No problem. I can deal with an old lady," Margaret said, "but you said 'a few complications.' What are the other ones?"

"Now you know how pleased I am that you've hooked up with Sam De Vere. Couldn't think of a finer person. He's so good for Paul and for you. You know, I was that upset when you took up with that computer fellow a while back."

"Gerald Toth? A mere flirtation, and you know it. He came to my aid and Dianne Stark's when we needed him. There was really nothing between us."

That was not strictly true. Margaret had been strongly attracted to Gerald, enough so that for a fleeting moment she had wondered if they had a future together. They had not, but at the time she had liked him very much. She hadn't seen him in months, though she'd heard that he still divided his time between the California headquarters of his company and the big apartment he'd taken in a classic old brownstone on East Seventy-fourth Street right here in Manhattan. "Well, go on. What's the complication?"

"This Miss Trenka who's coming to New York is here to do some business with Gerald Toth. If you're mindin' her, you could be meetin' up with him from time to time. Socializin' and things like that."

Margaret laughed. "I don't think a social encounter with Gerry would reignite any old flames." But just for a moment she remembered how handsome he was and how the touch of his hand had once set her heart beating fast. "I'm sure he must have a gorgeous model on each arm at all times of the day and night. I think I saw his name in Poppy Dill's column not too long ago. Lots of money and very good looks will attract sweet young things like nothing else."

Carolyn Sue hesitated. "Well, if you don't think it will cause any trouble between you and Sam . . . I surely would appreciate you handlin' Miss Trenka for me. Maybe you could take her to one of those benefit parties that everybody in New York thinks are so much fun. I'll bet she's never been to anythin' like them. I'll call Poppy, who will surely know if Toth is seein' somebody on a regular basis. It would ease my mind a whole bunch to know he's serious about one of these Yankee gold diggers."

The aged and eccentric Poppy Dill composed a society gossip column for one of the city's tabloid newspapers and knew everything about everybody who
was worth knowing about. If someone in high social
circles was misbehaving, having an affair, looting a
charity's treasury, or filing for divorce, some hint was
likely to appear in "Social Scene," along with the
names of every socially prominent person attending a
benefit ball for some important charity or an exclusive gallery opening or any of the hundreds of similar affairs that took place weekly during the New
York social season. If the parties involved in a scandal had paid proper court to her, the information
would remain undisclosed in the press, but Poppy
was known to use it to her advantage.

If Gerald Toth had a steady girlfriend, Poppy
would know all about her, from the city and state
where she was born to the shops where she bought
her undergarments and had her hair colored.

"Let me call Poppy," Margaret said. "I haven't
spoken with her for ages." She felt a tiny twinge of
guilt because she was suddenly very curious about
the current activities of Gerald Toth in spite of what
she'd told Carolyn Sue. She didn't want to hear news
of him through a Texas-accented third party. She
wanted to know from the Fount of All Gossip herself. "Uh, Carolyn Sue, when is this old lady coming
in from Connecticut?"

"Next week, I believe. On Monday. If you'd like,

I'll give you the telephone number of the man who's sending her and he could put you on to her to make plans. Poor Edward is a lovely man, you'll like him."

"Poor?"

"Jus' a figger of speech, honey. Ted lost the use of his legs years ago after some kind of innoculation went wrong, and he gets around in a wheelchair now. I suppose that's why Miss Trenka is comin' to New York instead of him. Even with those ramps they've put on all the sidewalk curbs, it can't be easy to move around the city in a wheelchair." So Carolyn Sue gave Margaret Ted Kelso's phone number and went off to prepare for her week at a luxurious spa in the desert. "We'll meet up for a good ol' gossip when I come back to the city, lookin' all toned and wrinkle-free, I promise. And if you have any problems with Miss Trenka, you just leave a voice-mail message at my Dallas number and I'll handle things from wherever I am." Carolyn Sue always managed to stay connected, whether being bathed in mud or pummeled by a masseuse.

The fog still embraced the tops of the tall buildings, Margaret noted as she peeked through the drapes. Whatever was she going to do with an aged woman from the suburbs? She'd only recently devoted a good deal of energy to keeping track of that difficult young woman from Dallas, at the request of Carolyn Sue, and now she had another of Carolyn Sue's responsibilities to mind.

Actually, Miss Trenka was more Gerald's responsibility, but she'd be willing to share hosting chores with him, if he didn't currently have a female partner to take up the burden of guiding the Trenka woman to Bloomingdale's and Ralph Lauren's boutique, down to the ferry to the Statue of Liberty and up Fifth Avenue to the Metropolitan Museum of Art. No, that wasn't quite right. Elderly ladies were not as enchanted by the prospect of Bloomingdale's cosmetic counters as younger women might be, and Miss Trenka might not even be up to long tramps through museums and subway rides to the tip of Manhattan. But she'd probably enjoy the Morgan Library and the Frick Collection. Steering an elderly lady around Manhattan was sure to be a chore, and she didn't have the funds to hire endless taxis, but that would be her only choice unless Gerald came up with a chauffeured vehicle. He could easily afford it, so she'd talk him into it.

She dialed the Connecticut number of Ted Kelso and explained who she was.

"I know your name, Lady Margaret, and I met your father, the Earl of Brayfield, once years ago. How is he getting on?"

"Thank you for inquiring, but alas, he died a few years back. My brother has the title now."

Ted chuckled. "You mean that mischievous little schoolboy I remember from my visit to Priam's Priory is an earl today? Doesn't seem possible. I don't remember a mischievous little girl, though."

"If you're referring to me, I had probably been

sent to the nursery to be taught manners by my nanny," Margaret said. "Perhaps we'll meet now that I have learned them." She wrote down Elizabeth Trenka's telephone number and said, "Don't warn her of my coming call. I need to look at my schedule to see when I'll be free to entertain her."

"I've arranged for her to dine with a business associate on Monday. Gerald Toth. You may have heard of him. I understand he's an active participant in the better New York social circles, to judge from the press coverage he receives."

Margaret blinked.

"Otherwise, I think she has no commitments," Ted Kelso was saying, "although she's probably making plans for things to do right now. She's quite independent, so I don't know that you need to go overboard in entertaining her."

"That's a relief. I can scarcely entertain myself."

All that remained was to call Poppy Dill to find out if there was any news of Gerald floating about the avenues of the East Side.

"Margaret, what a surprise! I can't talk long, I've got another of those damned deadlines to meet." Poppy sounded in good humor. "Terrible day, isn't it?"

Since it was well known that Poppy never ventured outside her apartment, which was not too many blocks from where Margaret resided on the Upper East Side, it was doubtful that she was referring to the fog.

"Terrible?"

"My dear, you haven't heard?"

Obviously Margaret hadn't heard anything, at least nothing that would warrant Poppy's breathless question.

"The stock market. It's down, down, down. People are beginning to worry. They hate to see their nest eggs diminish when there are so many things still to buy. I blame it on all these technology companies that have been hoodwinking us with their promises of wealth beyond imagining. Dot-coms, indeed. Things were far better when people could just invest in AT&T and be done with it."

"I suppose a declining stock market affects people like Gerald Toth," Margaret said, rather proud of herself for thinking this the perfect moment to bring up his name.

"Oh, certainly. He owns most of the stock in Xaviera Corporation, and if its value goes down, so does his net worth. On paper at least. But I imagine Gerald is well prepared for any stock market correction, as they see fit to call it."

"I haven't seen him in ages," Margaret said. "What do you suppose he's up to these days?"

"Do you mean who is he seeing?" Then Poppy went on without waiting for Margaret to answer. "Happily, he's given up Elinor Newhall. Well, she was entirely unsuitable. And Leila Parkins has gone back to California to work her wiles on Brad Pitt or Ben Affleck or another of those boy starlets. I can't tell them apart nowadays. But Leila was far too young for Gerald, in any case, although you have to admire her for trying."

A few years before Leila Parkins had managed to achieve certain heights as a much-reported-on debutante, but society and the general public had a way of turning its back on those who managed to allow the years to slip by without making a spectacular marriage to match their social position. Leila was supposedly attempting a career in films, or at least a cozy spot on the fringes of show business, probably something that didn't require much effort on her part. Gerald had had a brief fling with her, and he had once been commandeered by Elinor Newhall, a prominent hostess with a taste for handsome and rich men.

"He's been seen about town with—oh, cliché, cliché—a very attractive model on his arm. I think I mentioned it once in a column. She has only one name, of course. Brunetta, although she's actually a blonde. I've heard that she's quite bright, although that can't possibly be true from what I've seen of the modeling profession. She has a very promising career and all that. Very big in Europe. Brunetta has a contract with one of the big cosmetic firms to be their Face. I really have no idea whether Gerald is serious about her. I can't imagine what they have to talk about. He still keeps his apartment on East Seventy-fourth Street, so you could reach him there. I have his private number."

"It's all right. I have his number still. But why would I want to reach him?"

"Isn't that why you called? To find out what he's up to? Did you have a falling-out with Sam De Vere? Such a lovely man, so stable but so poor."

"Poppy . . ." Margaret said warningly.

"You have to look out for your future, Margaret. You're not getting any younger, and you need to get yourself settled with all the finer things of life at hand. Leila, who's a good twelve years younger than you, knows that very well, although she hasn't yet found exactly the right mate. Just trust me. I know how the world works."

"I do appreciate your concern, Poppy, but I'm not interested in rekindling something that didn't exist in reality. However, I may be required to meet Gerald shortly for reasons other than romance," Margaret said. "I have taken on the care and feeding of a woman who's coming in from Connecticut to meet with him. Carolyn Sue wants me to see that she's entertained. She's an . . . an older woman. I don't know anything more about her at present. I gather she's a retired businesswoman."

"How tedious for you, dear."

"I'll manage. At least she's not staying with me but at the Villa d'Este. Ah, Poppy. Are there any smallish charity events coming up that I could take her to? I mean, if she lives in retirement in Connecticut, she might find something like that amusing."

"Yes, but what part of Connecticut? Green's

Farms? Darien? Westport? If it's one of those places, she's probably quite blasé about social things. Well, I'll think of something for her. Now that the fall season is beginning, everyone is trying to capture the newly returned from summer holiday people before anyone else does."

"I really don't know where she's from," Margaret said. "I have the impression that she's not quite upper class. We'll find out soon enough. She's arriving on Monday, and I'm to ring her soon to see exactly what her plans are. After we've settled that, I can get on to Gerald if it seems necessary."

"When you do speak with him, remember to be gentle. Even if he's still got plenty of money, a downturn in the stock market tends to make men cranky."

CHAPTER 5

BEFORE SHE telephoned Miss Trenka, somewhere in Connecticut, or Gerald Toth, somewhere in Manhattan, Margaret fished around in a pile of fashion magazines near the chintz-covered sofa and found one with the latest portraits of the day's current hot models, helpfully labeled with their names. Among them was a picture of supermodel Brunetta, definitely blond, appallingly thin, with pouty too-full lips, a bosom that had probably been surgically enhanced, high cheekbones, and dark-lashed eyes. Very pretty, indeed.

Gerald certainly hasn't been taking her out to dinner much, she thought, and idly pinched the flesh of her thigh. It was rather more substantial than any visible part of Brunetta's slim body except for her voluptuous breasts.

She picked up the phone and dialed. It rang several times before a woman answered.

"Is that Miss Trenka?" Margaret thought she

heard a murmur of assent. "This is Lady Margaret Priam calling from New York."

"I beg your pardon. I do not believe I know a Lady Margaret."

"I'm calling at the request of Carolyn Sue Hoopes, who tells me you'll be visiting Manhattan next week and staying at Mrs. Hoopes's hotel, the Villa d'Este."

Miss Trenka hesitated. "Yes, that's correct, but I don't understand . . ."

"Ah, yes. My accent." Even after nearly a decade in the United States, Margaret's English accent remained.

"No, no. I mean, I don't understand why you would be calling me. I had no appointment with Mrs. Hoopes. My business is with . . . with someone else."

"Yes, Gerald Toth. But Carolyn Sue is to be out of town for a time, so she asked me to look after you, help you in any way I can. I'm merely calling to find out when you plan to be here so that I can make arrangements to . . . entertain you."

"That really isn't necessary," Betty said. "I have a little business with Mr. Toth, about whom you appear to know something, and I might take a bit of time to see some sights, but I really don't need looking after, although I do appreciate your offer."

Margaret liked the self-sufficient Miss Trenka already. "But it would be a pleasure. When will you be arriving?"

"On Monday in the afternoon. I shall take a taxi

from Grand Central to the hotel, so you needn't trouble yourself about that. I have an appointment to dine with Mr. Toth that evening, and I believe I will be meeting with him again on Tuesday."

"Then let's plan to have dinner on Tuesday evening and arrange then whatever you'd like to do during the rest of your visit."

"Truly, Lady Margaret, nothing needs to be arranged. However, I would be pleased to have dinner with you on Tuesday."

"Excellent. Then I will ring you at your hotel on Tuesday morning to suggest a time and place. Let me give you my telephone number in case there is anything I can do before then."

Margaret recited her number, then Betty said, "I don't imagine there will be anything I need, but I am grateful for your kindness." Then Betty spelled her name and said quite forcefully that her first name was Elizabeth, wondering how long it would be before this English lady decided to call her Betty.

Finally Margaret asked, "Miss Trenka, where is it in Connecticut that you live?"

"A town called East Moulton. It's not near anywhere you've probably heard of. Very small. And quaint. Good-bye until Tuesday."

At least elderly Elizabeth Trenka wasn't a grande dame lording it over the peasants in an exclusive enclave in Westport or Darien. She didn't sound that old either. Feisty in fact, no assistance needed.

* * *

Betty gazed thoughtfully at the phone she had just hung up, then frowned. Lady Margaret, indeed. She wondered if someone, Ted perhaps, was playing a joke, having persuaded some female friend capable of putting on an upper-class British accent to call her to make the trip to New York sound even more enticing. He needn't have bothered. She was already looking forward to it. The only thing that cast a slight shadow over the New York adventure was Ted's mention of possible wrongdoing in connection with this software program he was thinking about working on.

Well, she wasn't going to get involved in anything criminal, or even in helping to uncover something criminal, that was for certain. Now she needed to get organized.

Betty's trusted method of organization was to make a list, which she did as she ate a modest ham sandwich at the kitchen table:

Check my clothes.
Look up Xaviera Corporation on the Internet.
Make a list of questions for Ted.
Speak to Penny about the cat.
Buy cat food.
Find out who this Lady Margaret might be.

There wasn't much else to add. Penny had a key to her house in case of emergency, and she'd leave the hotel's number with her.

She wasn't leaving a very complicated life behind for a week, was she? Then she added: Call library. The librarian could be quite unpleasant if her volunteers failed to notify her of their pending absence. Ah, the most important thing of all: Note to nursing home. An attendant could tell Sid that she would be away for a few days and wouldn't be visiting next week.

She quickly decided against having her hair styled. She was quite capable of pinning her thick mop of hair up into a reasonably elegant bun on top of her head, or else she'd wear it in a heavy braid down her back. If that had been good enough for Edwards & Son, it would be good enough for Gerald Toth and his computer millions.

Her wardrobe was the first order of business. She had only worn her beautiful green satin jacket once, to the high school dance she'd chaperoned last spring, so she had that. And so with the jewelry Sid had given her, she was well prepared for an occasion requiring fancy dress. The business suits from her working days would be adequate for meeting Mr. Toth and taking little tours of the city, probably even for a night at the theater. Shoes were a problem. She had nothing like shoes for evening wear, but there were her old pumps she'd worn at the office for business meetings and, of course, her reliable sneakers for casual wear and long walks. She understood that athletic shoes were commonly worn by women traveling to and from work, perhaps to be better able to sprint away from urban predators. But New York was supposed to be much safer than it had been in the past, and besides, she hadn't sprinted in years, except for that one dark moment at Zig-Zag when capture was imminent and running was the best choice under the circumstances.

She decided to stop at Town & Country Fashions in East Moulton center after she went to the grocery store to stock up on cat food for Tina. Some nice frock might catch her eye and give her one more wining and dining option. Linda Rockwell wouldn't be there, of course, to advise her. She'd probably been replaced by some high school girl who wouldn't understand the needs and tastes of a woman Betty's age. She could handle it.

She decided that a note to the nursing home wasn't important after all. She had almost a week before she was to leave, so she'd drive up to see Sid before departing. She'd tell him herself that she'd be away the following week. She could make him understand better than any of the attendants, and she would certainly be able to tell whether he understood. She and Sid had always been able to communicate without a lot of words, and it still worked, even now when his mind was befogged by his illness and his speech was locked within him.

The fog had pretty much lifted by now, although the sky was still heavy with clouds. The roads wouldn't be quite as dangerous, so she went out to her trusty Buick and drove the scant mile to town.

Afternoons in East Moulton were as quiet as mid-mornings. Most people did their shopping early, so the supermarket was nearly empty. She picked out a week's worth of premium cat food, the kind that Tina was granted only on special occasions, and put a few items for herself in the cart. Wining and dining was a week off, after all, and a person had to eat in the meantime.

On the return trip she parked opposite Town & Country Fashions and wondered if she was being extravagant for no reason. After all, if something came up in New York that she didn't have the proper clothes for, there were hundreds of shops in the city where she could buy something. Nevertheless, she crossed Main Street and went in. She saw no saleswoman, only a short, balding man she thought was one of the owners.

"Can I help you, madam?"

"I'm mostly just looking," Betty said. "I have to go to New York on business and—"

"Our clothes for professional ladies are over here."

"I wasn't thinking so much of business attire. Rather, I expect I'll be entertained in the evenings and I wanted . . . something nice."

He looked up at her, as most men had to because she was usually so much taller than they. Then he squinted at her, looking her up and down. "Do you wear black?"

"Of course, if it's something I like."

"Nothing implied, madam, it's just that . . . um . . . mature ladies sometimes think that wearing black is a widow's statement. I've always believed that a simple black dress with nice accessories is suitable for almost any occasion. It's a bit too early in the season for velvet, I'm afraid, but we do have this nice silk in what would be your size." He grasped a hanger from one rack and swirled a long-sleeved black gown embroidered with bits of jet around the neckline for her inspection.

"I wasn't actually thinking of a floor-length dress," Betty said hesitantly, although she liked the look of the dress immediately. "I don't believe that formal wear is going to be necessary."

"Dear madam, this dress would be appropriate for both formal and casual affairs. People are wearing long dresses to just about everything nowadays. Indeed, I imagine that you will look so truly distinguished that no one will question your choice of outfit. Will you try it on?"

She certainly would, and had to agree, when she looked at herself in the mirror, that she did look quite distinguished, even if the sneakers peeking out from under the hem were slightly laughable.

"I'm an easy-to-please customer," she said after she'd changed back into her everyday clothes. "I'll take it."

"An excellent choice. You won't be disappointed," the salesman said as he took her credit card. "Ah, you're the Miss Trenka everybody talks about. I'm Howard Nestor, owner of Town & Country. We haven't found the right replacement for poor Linda Rockwell, so I've been handling the job since last spring."

"Very sad about Linda," Betty said. She hated to remember that particular East Moulton tragedy, and she certainly didn't want to talk about it now. She supposed that it was her involvement in the affair that gave reason for "everybody" talking about her. It was not something she wished to contemplate— people talking about her.

"I'm sure you'll enjoy the dress and have a wonderful time in New York. It's been years since I've had the chance to visit the city myself," Howard Nestor said. "Such electricity, all that culture, those interesting people. I lived there for quite a while when I was studying at the Fashion Institute of Technology." He ducked his head sheepishly. "At one time I considered becoming a designer myself but followed the trail to retail instead. Actually," he went on in almost a whisper, "I was asked to leave FIT because a classmate accused me of stealing his designs. It's not something I'm proud of, but it wasn't true. New ideas floated around and I had the misfortune to duplicate some of his—quite innocently, I assure you. But the powers that be claimed to recognize his unique touches in my designs, so there was nothing for me to do but leave under a cloud. Well, designing is a cutthroat business, and I'm probably just as well off here in East Moulton. And I have my other shop at the mall, so I do well enough." He had started off looking quite sad, but as he went on, a bit of defiance showed itself.

Betty blinked. He was lying, of course. She was certain that he had stolen the designs, but over the years he had convinced himself otherwise. She wondered why he was telling her his life story, but it wasn't surprising. People tended to confide in her, as though they understood instinctively that she wouldn't spread their tales.

Betty decided on one more stop, this time the pharmacy. She had a supply of the medication she used to alleviate the nagging arthritis that sometimes slowed her walk and taunted her with twinges of pain, but she had something else in mind. Molly Perkins, the phamacist's wife who ran the store, beamed when she saw Betty entering the store.

"Why, Betty Trenka, you never come by anymore except to pick up your Sunday *Times* or refill your prescription. We never have time for a good old gossip." Gossip was the fuel that powered Molly's engine.

"I don't need to buy much, Molly. Today I do need a little something." Betty hesitated, almost embarrassed to say the words. "I . . . I need some makeup. Not much," she added hastily. "A bit of face powder and a new lipstick." She didn't have an old lipstick, if the truth were told. "I have a business meeting in New York and I'll probably be going out some, and

I want to look . . . presentable. But I don't want a lot of fancy stuff. Not my style."

Molly almost dragged her to the cosmetics counter and began piling boxes and bottles on the counter. "Here's some nice foundation, very light, just right for your coloring. And I'd suggest this blusher to put some roses in your cheeks."

Betty firmly rejected eyeliner, eye shadow, and mascara but chose the blusher and a pale pink lipstick. She succumbed to the foundation, too, and also bought a fake tortoiseshell case containing face powder with a little brush for applying it. No shiny nose for Elizabeth Trenka.

"I'm so glad the fog is lifting," Molly said. "Couldn't see out my door to the end of the backyard for days. I was afraid someone would come creeping through the fog and murder me and I'd never know anyone was there, it was that thick. I suppose that's what happened to that poor girl they found dead on the beach. She was probably enjoying a stroll along the water and someone attacked her, just like that." Molly shook her head. "A jealous lover or a rival for a man's affections. You see that all the time on television. I'm surprised the authorities didn't call you in to investigate, Betty."

Betty laughed. "I don't think I'm a qualified investigator, Molly, in spite of having been able to figure out a few such matters in the past, and it's certainly not something that I'm interested in doing again.

They'll find out who did it eventually, if it wasn't just a terrible accident. People do fall and hit their heads, although I can't imagine why anyone would want to stroll on a beach at night in a heavy fog. It was just an accident."

Molly said firmly, "I don't believe it. She was supposedly a young, healthy woman, and they say they found bruises on her neck as though someone had forced her face into the water so that she drowned. They're saying she was a famous beauty and she was wearing an expensive ring. I can't wait to find out what really happened."

"If she was famous enough, you're sure to hear. Thanks for your help in choosing this . . . stuff. I'll tell you all about New York when I get back." Betty waved to Perk, the pharmacist, hidden away in the back with his bottles and boxes of medications.

Betty drove home, content that she was ready for anything she might encounter in New York. As soon as she'd hung up her new dress, she dashed across the field that separated her house from the Sakses' neat ranch-style house and knocked on Penny's door. The sun had made a watery appearance and the afternoon was quite warm and pleasant. The yellow and white chrysanthemums in Penny's garden glowed in the pale afternoon sunlight and as usual the smell of baking and fresh paint seeped out through the screen door.

"Come on in, Betty." Penny was never anything but perky and welcoming. "The boys are in the basement playing computer games, so they won't disturb us. Want some coffee? Pop? I think I have some iced tea in the fridge." The slim, pretty young woman in jeans and a man's old shirt opened the refrigerator door and produced a pitcher. "See? I'm ready for anything. I guess iced-tea season is almost over though. Pretty soon I'll be making mulled cider and hot chocolate. Oh, and I just found some darling mugs that will be perfect for hot chocolate. Little snowmen and winter scenes."

"Iced tea would be lovely," Betty said, and started toward a bright red chair near the kitchen table.

"Oops! Don't sit in that one. The paint isn't quite dry yet. Let's go into the living room. I've finally managed to remove all the Pokémon items, radio-controlled cars, and Lego pieces, so for once it's habitable."

"I can't stay but a minute," Betty said. The tea was strong and lemony, and not too sweet. "As usual, I've come to ask a favor. I have to go to New York next week on business for Ted, and I was wondering if the boys could take on the job of feeding Tina morning and night while I'm away. I'll pay them something for their trouble."

"No problem," Penny said. "And you don't need to pay them. It's good for them to understand they have to help out their neighbor whenever they can."

"Little boys like to have a bit of extra cash," Betty said. "I know that even if I don't know much about children."

"Why, you know lots about them. You were so good when you substituted in the school office. I don't know what would have happened in the end if you hadn't understood what was going on. Tommy and I and the whole town will always be grateful."

"That's an old story," Betty said, "and best forgotten. So they'll handle Tina. She won't be grateful, I promise you, but I'll leave the cans of food stacked on the counter. One in the morning, one at night. Keep her water bowl filled and let her out to play once a day only. It's far too much food for her, I know. She just keeps getting fatter and meaner, but it's the only way I know how to handle her. I'm leaving on Monday and will be back the following Sunday."

"What is it you'll be doing for Ted? I never quite understood what he does to support himself, but he seems to keep busy."

"It's some kind of computer business he wants me to look into."

"I'm impressed," Penny said. "You know about computers?"

"I don't. Just what I learned on the job at Edwards & Son. Ted merely wants me to interview a prospective business associate."

"They don't have telephones anymore? The associate couldn't travel to East Moulton?"

"I believe when one is very, very rich, and very important and successful, people go to one rather than the other way around."

"Sounds intriguing. Is it Bill Gates?"

"No, a man named Gerald Toth."

Penny's eyes opened wide. "No kidding? I've read stuff about him in the gossip columns. He's always being seen with some famous or beautiful woman on his arm. Greg's mentioned him as well, but only in terms of his computer business. I think Greg even bought stock in Toth's company, although I was just hearing on the news that technology stocks have gone way down in the past couple days." She laughed. "Well, it couldn't have been a very big investment, we don't have a lot of loose money to toss into the stock market. Say, did you see that thing on television about that poor woman who was murdered on the beach? Gave me quite a chill. There's a long story about the case in tonight's paper. I've heard of the place where it happened." Penny refilled Betty's glass.

"We like to take the boys down to the shore to one of the state parks at least once every summer. This Redding's Point is right next to our favorite park. The boys just love the water. So does Greg. He keeps talking about buying a powerboat, but I put my foot down on that one. Imagine what the upkeep is. Anyhow, I make a big picnic lunch and we sometimes spend the whole weekend camping out. We have the greatest time. Now, Betty, you can go off and have a good time yourself, and don't worry about a thing."

"Before I go, I'll leave the number of the hotel where I'll be staying. And I'll probably be going up to see Sid Edwards before I leave. He gets restless if I don't show up at least once a week."

"How's he doing?" Betty had explained to Penny about the man she had worked with for so many years and the stroke that had felled him, but she had never gone into details about their relationship with Penny.

"He's . . . surviving. I know he wants to live and get better, but the doctors say he could have another stroke at any time, and that one would finish him." Betty put down her glass of tea, wanting to go home before she became emotional about Sid and then would have to share even more personal things with Penny.

"Be sure to give our number to the nursing home, so we can get in touch with you if anything happens," Penny said. "Not that I expect it, but it's best to be prepared. And, Betty, I think I do know how you feel about him. You can't hide that kind of attachment. But I want you to enjoy yourself. I know you like to keep active. My, New York! I'd love to go for a weekend, but it's damned hard to find anybody who's willing to look after my pack of devils."

The pack decided to make itself known because a volley of shouts and bangs erupted from the lower level. Betty took the opportunity to leave as Penny raced to the basement door to put out some Nintendo-based wildfire.

The sun was starting to set, and she seemed to feel

a dampness in the air that suggested the fog would once again creep back to turn the world gray in the morning.

But tomorrow Betty wouldn't feel gray. She had a job to do.

CHAPTER 6

ONCE AGAIN the silent fog crawled along the East Coast in the early morning as masses of warm and cold weather clashed high in the heavens and spawned a great gray cloud that settled cozily around Betty Trenka's house in Connecticut and swaddled Margaret Priam's apartment tower in Manhattan. It crept up the broad avenues of New York City and swirled east and west along the cross streets. It covered Central Park, making ghosts of the trees and filling up the underpasses on the cross-park roadways. The few early-morning walkers on East Seventy-fourth Street were mere shadows in the misty hours of the morning, occasionally caught in the headlights of taxis fetching and carrying eager workers to their offices or returning worn-out clubland revelers to their homes.

Gerald Toth had had a late night himself, gently pursuing his current love interest, Brunetta, the internationally renowned model whose slim silhouette had graced the fashion runways from New York to

Paris to Milan. Brunetta, however, had chosen to play hard to get, so Gerald had finally left her at her own door and returned home to his comfortable, indeed luxurious, rented apartment, wishing that the dawn would find him back home at his even more comfortable Woodside, California estate with the sun rising on his well-manicured garden and glossy stretch of lawn, where a breakfast table stood under the deep shade of a grandiflora magnolia.

He was not pleased to have been spurned by Brunetta, because he was absolutely certain that he was wildly attractive to all women, in appearance, in personality, and most of all in his bank accounts. He couldn't figure her out but suspected that she had taken up with some other man. Of course, she made a good living by just showing up to be draped with elegant clothes and photographed, but there was much more to life than being beautiful. Didn't she understand that she needed a lot more money than what she earned from modeling to have all the things she desired? And here he was, in a position to give them to her. He couldn't think of any other man with his kind of resources. Not even Donald Trump. Brunetta, he had to admit, was seriously lacking intellectually in many respects, but she certainly knew the value of a dollar or a great many dollars. He didn't understand her, but who pretended to understand a child?

Gerald was also not pleased to see the foggy day outside his building. Warmth and sun were the elements that suited him. He had taken a buffeting on the stock market only the day before, and like any businessman of his stature, he had other problems and even enemies to deal with. He decided he would do nothing today, put off any business calls, meet no one, until the weather gave him some support. So he almost didn't answer the ringing phone. But it was his private number, given out to only a few close friends. It might be important. It might even be Brunetta, come to her senses. He answered.

It wasn't Brunetta at all. In any case, it was too early for her to be awake if she wasn't working, and if she was off somewhere posing before a camera, she wouldn't have the time to call him. It was a man whose raspy voice he didn't quite recognize.

"I've gotcha now, Toth."

"Who is this? Elliott? How'd you get this number?"

"If I was that stinkin' little thief Elliott Wolfson, I'd kill myself. But I'm not, so I'm gonna kill you. Film at eleven. You'll be hearin' from me soon, Toth." The caller hung up. Gerald stared at the phone. If he wasn't mistaken, he'd just received a death threat. A mild one to be sure, but a threat nonetheless. If it wasn't Elliott, then he thought he knew who it was. Ivor Beame, of course, certainly would wish him dead.

When the phone rang again soon afterward, he hesitated, then finally answered. There was still a chance it could be Brunetta.

"Hullo, Gerald. It's Margaret Priam."

"Margaret, what a surprise. How nice to hear your voice on this gloomy day." Here was another female who had not been overwhelmed by his blandishments. What had happened to his golden touch with women, anyhow? He decided that business worries had worked to lessen his appeal. He briefly allowed himself to think back to a time when he'd found perfect love. Xaviera had adored him, but then she had betrayed him and vanished. He'd take her back in a second.

"Isn't it depressing? I look out and imagine cloaked villains creeping through the fog to set upon the innocent with sharp daggers."

"I don't think that sort of thing happens in New York nowadays, although one might be set upon by renegade rap musicians. To what do I owe the pleasure of your call?"

Margaret didn't quite know how to begin, lest Gerald think she'd been doggedly gathering information about him. After all, she'd only seen him a few times quite a while ago, and it really hadn't been serious, had it? "Quite an odd reason, as it happens. You know Carolyn Sue Hoopes, of course."

"I do. Ben Hoopes is a pal of mine. We used to do a bit of hunting and fishing when I could spare the time, and we've even done some business together over the years. Carolyn Sue is quite a character."

"Mmmm, she is. She's also fond of asking favors of her friends, who are willing to comply since, as you know, she does many favors in return. It seems she's asked me to entertain a lady who's coming to New York to meet with you in a week or so. A Miss Elizabeth Trenka. I have no idea what your business with her may be, but I gather she's somewhat elderly. I didn't want to trouble to make elaborate plans for her if you already have done so."

Gerald didn't answer for a moment, and Margaret wondered if he even knew who she was talking about. Then he said, "Miss Trenka is an associate of a man I've asked to do some independent consulting work for my company. I really had planned nothing for her visit except for some discussions that Ted Kelso seems to think are necessary. Oh, I've promised to take her to dinner on Monday to be polite. And I'd be especially delighted to have you join us."

"And I've arranged to dine with her next Tuesday. Won't you join us?"

"Wonderful idea, though I wonder if I need to eat with Miss Trenka daily. I've been wanting to see you for a long time, but I've been—"

"Seen about with a supermodel or two?" Margaret laughed. "No secrets in this town, Gerald. I have Miss Trenka's phone number, so I'll ring her and tell her the plans have changed. I get you free of your dinner on Monday and the three of us will dine instead on Tuesday. I haven't picked a spot yet, but I'll ring you on Tuesday and tell you where to meet us. Any preferences?"

"Somewhere fairly quiet, I think. I won't have met

the lady before, and it might be easier to get acquainted if the surroundings are subdued. Cozy. I'd enjoy sitting knee to knee with you." Margaret couldn't help but feel a tingle of excitement. Gerald was magnetic, no doubt about it. She tried to conjure up an image of De Vere, but to no avail. All she could picture was Gerald Toth and those gorgeous blue eyes of his.

Then he said, "It's nearly a week until next Tuesday. Is there time in your busy schedule to do something fun with me before then?" If he chose the right spot, people would see them together and start talking. Brunetta would certainly hear of it, and her icy heart might start to heat up with jealousy. A titled lady, after all, was a class or two above a mere hanger for designer clothes.

"I just might be able to find time for you, Gerald."

"Saturday evening then? I'll send a car for you around seven. I'll be interested to hear what you've been up to—and Mrs. Stark, after all that trouble."

Dianne Stark was Margaret's best friend in New York. A former flight attendant who had married well and produced a lovely child, she and Margaret often did the social circuit together, served on the same committees, and confided in each other. Maybe she would also be willing to assist in the care and feeding of Elizabeth Trenka.

"Dianne's doing well. She's studying to become a home aide for disabled people. She wants to do something useful with her life rather than just be the wife of a rich man and a social butterfly. I wish I could find the same kind of purpose in my own life."

"You will. Ah, I'm afraid I have to run. There's someone at the door." Could it be Ivor Beame? Making good on his threat rather promptly?

"I hope it's not one of the cloaked villains with a dagger in his hand," Margaret said.

Gerald sounded remarkably serious as he said, "And I hope the same. Until Saturday then."

Gerald Toth did not keep a servant in New York, so he went reluctantly down the stairs from his second-floor apartment to answer the door himself. His mind raced through the rather long list of people who might want to kill him if it was not Ivor on the other side of the door.

He wondered if it might be Elliott. Elliott Wolfson had been a renowned programmer for years at Ivor Enterprises and had only come over to Xaviera Corporation a few months earlier without at first explaining why he'd abandoned Ivor Beame. Gerald soon learned the reasons. Elliott had decided to sell his programming genius to a higher bidder and he had something else for sale.

At first they'd discussed in general terms new directions for Xaviera's software. Gerald had long toyed with the idea of developing what was called an Enterprise Resource Planning system, which would consolidate the separate systems of major companies, especially those merging with other companies, to create a streamlined, efficient system. It was a huge programming undertaking. Then, out of the blue, Elliott had offered Xaviera a massive ERP program he claimed he'd developed himself. Well, Elliott had the genius to do it, and Gerald had been so excited about the possibilities that he failed to think the matter through. Then he realized that Elliott couldn't possibly have had the financial resources to create the system on his own, that he had to have written the program for his former employer, and thus it was stolen property.

By the time Gerald realized what he had and where it had originated, complex and expensive machinery had been turned on and its force was too great to halt. The pirated software was on the brink of coming onto the market, and the business world had already heard about Xaviera Corporation's Wyatt Enterprise Resource Planning system. Toth's public relations people had started the rumor that it was far better than any of the similar ERP systems that had been developed and were beginning to be used by big businesses to blend and manage all their resources. The business press and the computer magazines had picked up the rumor and embellished it. The market was eagerly anticipating its release.

It was almost as good a promotion job as Bill Gates had done for Windows. All that was needed was some final testing before Xaviera could start to rake in the millions of dollars each system would cost. Ted Kelso was being hired to do that, and now

Gerald hoped Ted would validate the fact that the programming code did not announce it could only have come from Elliott's mind, financed by Ivor Enterprises. If necessary, Ted could see to it that Elliott's telltale style was erased so that Ivor Beame wouldn't be able to accuse Xaviera of theft. Gerald was planning to pay Ted Kelso a lot of money if he could confirm that the code came from Xaviera's programmers alone.

Well, Elliott might suddenly be feeling guilty about his theft, but murder seemed a pointless expiation. It was much more likely that Ivor Beame was ready to punish Gerald with death for seeking to profit from Elliott's crime. Ivor was ruthless enough, and murder was not beyond the scope of his imagination, but he wouldn't do the deed himself. He'd send an emissary to carry out his dirty work. The doorbell rang again, this time impatiently.

Gerald slowly turned the dead-bolt locks and opened the door. He felt the sweat in his armpits and a trembling sensation in his stomach, ready to die at the hands of Ivor's hit man if that was what his fate would be.

He faced a dark-skinned muscular young man in tight black spandex and a purple windbreaker with a bicycle helmet under his arm.

"Hey, man. JayCee Couriers. Got an envelope for Gerald Toth." He handed over a brown manila envelope.

"That's me," Gerald said. "Where do I sign?" He

scrawled his name on the receipt and closed the door, breathing heavily. The envelope was slim, but he felt it gingerly. No indication of an explosive device inside, able to blow off his hand or sharp nails to pierce his skin and heart. So he wasn't going to be blown away by a letter bomb. At least not now.

He carried the envelope to his study and placed it on the desk. No return address, just his name and address printed in block letters. He found that his legs were trembling and he felt a bit nauseated, so he sat down and stared at the envelope. He was reluctant to open it, even if he was pretty sure it wouldn't explode. It could only mean trouble, even if it solely contained more threats from Ivor. Suddenly he went to his bedroom and found a pair of heavy driving gloves, some sunglasses to protect his eyes, and a heavy sweatshirt to pull on over the Ralph Lauren Polo shirt he was wearing. Back in his study, he carefully slit the end of the manila envelope with a sharp letter opener, but nothing happened. There appeared to be only three sheets of paper inside.

He was so relieved that he hadn't been maimed or killed that he put the envelope aside again, to read what it contained later.

Then he decided he'd better call both his New York and California attorneys to prepare them for possible litigation if Ted Kelso didn't do his job properly. But he wouldn't go into details, not yet. He wouldn't even mention that Ivor had threatened to kill him. Computer guys preferred bytes to blood anyhow. Naturally, both attorneys were unavailable, so he left voice-mail messages for them to return his calls, cursing the fact that literally no one was ever at his desk when he made an important phone call.

He closed his eyes and tried some stress-reduction and relaxation techniques that had been helpful in the past. Think of something pleasant. Well, he had dinner with Margaret Priam to look forward to. She had intrigued him from their first meeting, but it was odd to think that his business with Ted Kelso had been an instrument for bringing them together again, via Miss Elizabeth Trenka, whatever her particular game might be. He began to feel more relaxed as he breathed deeply and even dozed a bit as he sensed the tension seeping away.

It was going to be all right, he was sure, and with the many millions Xaviera would earn from the Wyatt ERP system, he'd arrange to compensate Elliott in such a way that he wouldn't be aware of where his windfall came from. And he'd have his New York secretary who came in occasionally to handle correspondence buy Margaret an expensive trinket from Tiffany or the like. Women liked that sort of thing, and Gladys loved to go shopping with his money.

Which restaurant should he take Margaret to so that Brunetta would be sure to hear about it? He wasn't as up on all the hot dining spots as he should be. He decided they'd try Keith McNally's new Pastis, which he had heard about from Brunetta herself. Somehow he'd manage a reservation even if the

place didn't take reservations. He was rich and famous, Margaret had a title. They'd get in.

By late in the afternoon he knew he had to look at
the contents of the envelope that had been delivered.
Not unexpectedly, it was a message from Ivor Beame,
even though it wasn't signed. One sheet was a short,
typed note.

> You won't get away with it, Toth. I
> know you're having the program tested,
> and I know who's doing it. I'll see you in
> court—or in your grave. All the best.

The second sheet was a page ripped from a glossy
magazine with a series of photographs of glossy persons attending social events in the city. Among them
was an indistinct shot of Gerald Toth and the beautiful Brunetta, who certainly knew how to keep her
best profile forward when a camera was in sight. He
couldn't remember where they'd been, some party
honoring a book publication, he thought. She'd been
so delighted to be mixing with "smart people like authors." Dear dumb Brunetta. Less pleasing to note:
Someone had defaced the photo with a red X across
Brunetta's face. He glanced at the third sheet. This
was a newspaper clipping, a story about a woman
found dead, possibly murdered, on a beach in Connecticut. Someone had circled in red "seeking anyone
who knew the dead woman, Jane Xaviera Corvo."
Gerald blinked, then felt a stinging in his eyes, but

the thought of actual tears was unacceptable. He drew a deep breath. Xaviera, his Xaviera, was gone forever. How could he have missed seeing the story? Well, the *Times* didn't usually cover sensational murders, and he seldom bothered with the *New York Post* or the *Daily News,* which did.

So Ivor was threatening Gerald's lady friends as well as the man himself. Had he had poor Xaviera killed? He slumped in a chair. The loss of Xaviera was painful, but she'd left him and he'd tried to suppress any lingering feelings about her. He hoped no one would connect her with him. Bad for business.

The last straw of the day was the policeman who showed up at his door. This time he didn't hesitate to open it, expecting to see another messenger on his doorstep with one more threatening note.

"Mr. Gerald Toth?" Gerald nodded and the man introduced himself as an emissary of the Connecticut State Police. "They're contacting people who knew Jane Corvo. It's been reported that she worked for you."

Gerald nodded again and brought the policeman up to his apartment. "She did, briefly. I just learned of her death," Gerald said. "Someone sent me a newspaper clipping. It was a shock, let me tell you. A fine person, not the kind to . . . to . . ."

"Get killed? When did you last see Miss Corvo?"

"Shouldn't I have my lawyer present?"

"Do you need legal advice, Mr. Toth? I'm not

accusing you of anything. We're just trying to trace her movements in the last few months."

"I haven't seen her in months. She used to work for me at my California headquarters when I was just starting my business. She worked in administration. I do admit that we fell in love, and I was foolish enough to name my company after the name she used. Xaviera. She was a lovely young woman, but she decided to leave me."

"And why was that?"

Gerald remembered that it was around the time that Elliott Wolfson had shown up at the Xaviera offices with the ERP program under his arm, in a manner of speaking. Xaviera and Elliott had become buddies, although he was a typical computer geek in plaid shirts and wrinkled khakis. He'd see them sitting out in the little garden behind the building while he smoked his pipe, forbidden indoors. They'd have their heads together, talking seriously about who knew what. It certainly couldn't have been about software, because Xaviera had known next to nothing about the subject.

He'd tried to wean her away from Elliott by taking her on holiday trips to Big Sur, to San Francisco, to Las Vegas. He'd bought her jewelry himself, not asking one of the secretaries to do it for him. He'd once given her a beautiful ring with a huge tanzanite surrounded by diamonds. He'd thought of it as a pre-engagement ring. Then had come the blowup. He was assuming too much; he was fencing her in, trapping her in a life she didn't want against her will. She was a free spirit. She didn't care how much money he had. She wasn't going to stand for it anymore. She was leaving. And she left. And soon thereafter Elliott had gone back east, with Gerald Toth's promises of a big payoff for bringing the ERP system to him. Gerald had always thought Elliott had left to follow Xaviera, but he couldn't be sure.

"Mr. Toth? I asked you why she left you." The policeman was still there.

"I'm sorry. I was thinking back to our final parting. She . . . she said I was too possessive and she wanted to be free. I don't understand women. I gave her everything."

"Do you know where she went when she left you?"

"I think she came here to New York. To work for Ivor Beame. That might be the biggest betrayal of all. Beame is my major competitor in business."

"And you never saw her again."

"Never. I suggest you ask Ivor Beame about her. He saw her much more recently than I did."

The policeman asked him to account for his whereabouts the previous weekend.

Fortunately, Gerald had been right there in the city. Brunetta had not been free to see him all weekend because she'd been out of town shooting a magazine layout. She probably wouldn't be of a mind to offer an alibi anyhow, but he had accepted invitations for social affairs on both Saturday and Sunday. The hostess at each event could testify to his appearance.

The policeman seemed satisfied and promised to inform him if the murderer was discovered. He also assured Gerald that Jane Corvo's mother was handling the funeral arrangements and that there was nothing that needed to be done.

When the policeman departed, Gerald pondered what to do. Xaviera was dead, but there was still the defaced picture of Brunetta with its implied warning. Finally, well into the evening, he called Brunetta's cell phone, not expecting to reach her. She often turned it off while partying.

But she answered. There was a lot of noise in the background—voices and music—so he assumed she was out on the town with the rest of the Beautiful People.

"I don't want to alarm you, Bru, but be very careful, don't be alone, don't answer the door to strangers."

"What are you talking about? Who is this?"

"It's Gerald, you ninny. Somebody's been threatening me and implying that you're in danger, too." He hoped the words weren't too difficult for her. "Just be very careful. I'll check in with you tomorrow."

"I have a shoot tomorrow. All day. There're always lots of people around. Photographers, stylists, hair people, makeup people, the client's people. You know, like, lots of people."

"Whatever. Just be careful. Call me if you're worried."

He heard her speaking to someone else. "Be right with you, sweetie. Meet you at the bar." Her attention span, always brief, had lapsed.

Gerald sighed and disconnected. Then he called an agency he'd used in the past and demanded that a bodyguard be sent around to his place immediately. The agency was happy to oblige Mr. Toth and assured him that Sonny Arcola would be on his doorstep in a matter of minutes for as long as he was needed.

Gerald waited until the brawny Sonny arrived in good time, explained that he'd been threatened and just wanted someone in the apartment that night for protection. Sonny shrugged, found an easy chair to his liking in the study, and turned on the TV. He was very large and wore a holstered gun under his jacket, which promised sufficient protection. Gerald left him watching a game show while he went to his desk to reread the story about the murder in Connecticut and to review some paperwork. He wondered if he ought to call Ted Kelso, to warn him that a bit of unpleasantness might be looming, even though the program hadn't yet been sent to him. Ivor thought he knew who would be doing the testing, but he wouldn't know if Ted would reveal the truth about the pirated software. If anything happened to Ted, there were plenty of others Gerald could turn to for the same desired result.

He'd talk to Ted when he'd seen this associate of his. Maybe Miss Elizabeth Trenka could carry the warning along with the set of CDs he was sending to Ted. He was sure Ted could be trusted to be on his side. Money bought a lot of loyalty.

CHAPTER 7

BETTY ALWAYS saved the Sunday *New York Times* she picked up each week at the pharmacy until she had the new one in hand. So she got out the one from the previous Sunday to look through the Arts & Leisure section, to see if there was anything happening she might want to see. Musicals, dramas, some new movies that hadn't reached the multiplex at the mall, but she had never been a big moviegoer. There appeared to be a musical version of *King Lear,* of all things. Called *The Serpent's Tooth,* it was still in previews. She could easily imagine such a thing closing before it even officially opened, but the very idea of it had a certain bizarre appeal, and the stars were quite well known. Maybe she'd give it a try. She scanned the list of upcoming performances at the Metropolitan Opera and New York City Opera, but she had never succumbed to the lure of high singing, even though Ted liked to play selections during the dinners he cooked for her. She'd rely on Lady Margaret to guide her.

What sort of lady was she? With that accent, she had to be English. Betty opened her fat *Random House Dictionary* and looked up *lady*. She got past the first definitions and read, "The proper title of any woman whose husband is higher in rank than baronet or knight, or who is the daughter of a nobleman not lower than an earl, although the title is given by courtesy also to the wives of baronets and knights."

So her Lady Margaret might be the wife of Sir Somebody or the daughter of a nobleman who was at least an earl. Then she looked up *earl* and found that such a person was a rank above a viscount and just below a marquis. This was almost better than an Italian-American princess, as Mrs. Hoopes was alleged to be. English titles were real, but she wasn't so sure about the Italians, who had, after all, thrown out their king. Still, she would love to be able to mention in passing to Molly at the pharmacy that she'd been visiting her friend, the nobleman's daughter, Lady Margaret, plus an Italian princess.

"Elizabeth," she told herself firmly, "don't go giving yourself airs. Whoever she is, she's just a person." But just the same she'd ask Ted if he knew anything about her.

While Betty was planning her trip, Ted was planning his own next step, and that consisted of a long telephone conversation with his potential employer, Gerald Toth.

"I'll see that you get these CDs by next week," Gerald said. "There are several of them. It's a big program. And I'll need your results as soon as possible thereafter. What if I send them back next week with your assistant, Miss Trenka?"

"I think you can rely on Federal Express to get them to me promptly," Ted said.

"I just don't like the idea of handing over a package to an unknown person and having a lot of other unknown persons conveying it to you. It's pretty valuable."

"Are you worried that the person who lost it will try to retrieve it?" Ted was almost sorry he'd mentioned the dubious origins of the CDs, which were, after all, pure speculation.

"I don't know what you mean, Kelso. Everything is strictly legal. I suppose you've seen that garbage about theft. I acquired the program legitimately. It never belonged to Ivor Beame. I had my own people working on it. If you have the slightest hesitation about working for me, I can easily find someone else. But remember, the amount of money I'm paying you is generous."

"No problem, Gerry. Miss Trenka is extremely reliable, probably better than FedEx, and I didn't mean to imply anything about the program, no matter what people are saying."

"I don't need comforting words from the likes of you, Kelso. I need results. And by the way, somebody has been sending me threats. I'd advise you to be careful."

Ted frowned at the now-silent phone. He was quite accustomed to bad-tempered executives, but he was glad he was sending Elizabeth to spy on the personality landscape for him. She was capable of seeing beyond mere bad temper. Since he'd never actually met Gerald Toth, it was good to know that someone would have the opportunity to look him in the eyes. Those legendary blue eyes.

He'd noticed Betty drive away and return, then saw her cross the field to Penny Saks's house. Once again the fog had lifted by late afternoon, but the sun was feeble, as though its energy was fading as summer departed and autumn arrived. He sat beside his front windows for quite a long time, watching the shadows of the pines lengthen and the sky darken as dusk descended. He was convinced that the ERP program Toth wanted him to look at was stolen property, and he wondered what he would do when the evidence of piracy was right before him on the screen. He didn't think he was capable of being a party to the crime, but should he keep silent and give Toth the validation he wanted? Or should he inform the authorities of his suspicions? Well, he needed proof first and then he'd decide.

Suddenly, he sat up in his wheelchair and leaned forward. A car with unlit headlights was proceeding slowly along Timberhill Road, as if someone was trying to read names on the mailboxes. His box didn't have his name on it, merely the street number, but the car slowed down to a bare crawl as it passed his house. He was glad the room was darkened, so no one could see him sitting by the window. Then the car sped up and headed toward East Moulton center, not bothering to check either Betty's mailbox or the Sakses'. The driver must have found what he or she was looking for.

He couldn't help but feel uneasy. Toth had warned him to be careful. He was so defenseless, trapped in the wheelchair, although there was an antique Civil War officer's sword propped beside the fireplace. A lot of good that would do him if some goon from Ivor Beame's company chose to invade his home. The best he could do now was lock his doors, set the burglar alarm, and retreat to his bedroom. Since he'd done nothing about the Xaviera software and didn't even have it yet, what would be the point of harming him? And as Toth had said to him, if Ted didn't do the testing, there were a lot of other people who would gladly take Xaviera's money and do the job, although perhaps not as well as Ted, who carried a lot of clout in this particular world. And he knew Elliott Wolfson's programming techniques intimately and would recognize his hand in creating the code. Elliott had been Ivor Beame's employee. There were any number of other telltale clues to indicate whether a program had been pirated.

Ted refused to worry about the strange car. If anyone tried to get into his house—and for what purpose really?—he had both Betty's number and the resident state trooper's number on speed dial. No problem so far. Still, he didn't want to put Betty in any kind of danger, even though she appeared to be quite capable of taking care of herself. When many millions of dollars were involved in terms of development and future sales, as would be the case with Gerald Toth's Enterprise Resource Planning system, people were likely to take serious steps to protect their investment and their future earnings.

Later that night the phone rang in Ted Kelso's house. He hesitated before answering it, then finally picked it up.

"Is this the Edward Kelso who used to spend summers at Redding's Point in Connecticut?" It was a man's voice, unrecognized by Ted.

"Who is calling?"

"I'm looking for Ted Kelso. I'm an old friend. It's important." The man's voice sounded urgent, a little uneasy. "All I'm asking is if you're him."

"I need to know who's calling before I answer that."

A sigh. "Stan Thurlow."

"Stan! How are you doing? It's been years."

"Thank God it's you, Ted. I've been calling all over the state of Connecticut to find you. There are a lot of E. Kelsos around, but I finally remembered which town your family came from and I took a chance that you were still there."

"My family's gone, but I decided to stay put. What's the problem, Stan?"

"It's kind of a crazy thing. We had this . . . incident a couple days ago. You maybe read about it. A dead girl on the beach. My kids found the body when they were scavenging on the beach."

"What are you doing in Redding's Point at this time of year? I thought you lived in Springfield."

"I moved the wife and the boys here a few years ago. I've always loved the point and being near the water, so I winterized the old house and got a job at a small company inland a few miles. Foreman of the plant. I finally got my own sailboat."

"What about this dead woman then? I did read about it. They didn't seem to know who she was."

"They do now. Some trampy, hippie dame from California. Jane Corvo, but she called herself Xaviera. A state cop who's a friend told me."

The mention of that name jolted Ted. An unusual female name and the same as one of the biggest corporations around. "Did this cop tell you anything else?"

"She used to work for some computer company called . . ."

Ted smiled.

". . . called Ivor Enterprises. You ever hear of it?"

"Yes," Ted said slowly. "I have heard of it, but that can't be right."

"I only know what I was told," Stan said. "But here's my problem, and I don't know what to do. I remembered that you used to talk about computers and all that science-fiction stuff before anybody knew they were going to be a big thing someday, so I figured you could help me out."

Ted wondered when Stan would get to the problem. He'd always been one to skirt around an issue rather than come right to the point. "Go on," he said.

"When the boys found the girl lying there in the tidal pool—you remember that pile of rocks at the end of the beach near the Castle cottage? Anyhow, one of the little devils spotted a silver disc or something in the rocks and took it away with him before the cops came. They thought it was some kind of music CD, but it wouldn't play, so they stuck it away somewhere, but they felt guilty, so they finally confessed to me. I don't know anything about computers, but I know it's a computer disc. So I thought maybe you could give me an opinion before I go to the cops with it. I don't want Pete and Jack to get into trouble, and if it's nothing, then I won't even bother to mention it to them."

"You've got the disc there with you? Does it say anything on it?"

"Not much. There's a big X on it and then in what looks like Roman numerals just III slash IV. Looks to me like it means three of four."

"Stan," Ted said seriously, "put the disc away somewhere safe. I'm going to drive down to Redding's Point in a couple of days to have a look. And,

Stan, tell the boys not to talk about it, and if you see any strangers around the place, be careful."

"I did see a car on the right-of-way the night of the murder—you remember, that stretch of land that leads to the beach. I saw two people, one of them I know was a woman. Probably the dead woman. I did tell the cops about that. Since then I have seen a car I don't recognize a few times just driving around the roads. Sort of aimless. And there was a woman I didn't know walking along the beach the other day, kicking over piles of seaweed, like maybe she was looking for something. These artistic types are always looking for driftwood that would make a nice lamp. That's all. Redding's Point is pretty lonely this time of year, so you notice. When do you think you'll come?"

"I have to drive a friend to New Haven to catch a noon train on Monday. I could drive back along the turnpike to you after that."

"I'll be at work," Stan said, "but I'll tell my wife to give you the disc. I don't have a computer here for you to try it out, though."

"I'll bring it back here to East Moulton," Ted said. "And I'll let you know what I find out. Sure hate to miss seeing you."

"You're not missing much. I'm the same old Stan. Less hair, a few extra pounds. Here's my phone number in case you need to get in touch with me. And thanks, Ted. You always know what to do."

"Like the time old lady Morton called the cops when we were having a picnic on the island because she thought we were drinking beer and ravishing girls?"

"Hey, you buried the beer cans before they got there and then gave 'em hot dogs and Cokes and talked 'em into singing songs around the bonfire."

"We only had two cans of beer for the ten of us, remember," Ted said. "And we weren't driving, just rowing back from the island at low tide. We could have walked across the bay, the tide was so low that night."

"Yeah, almost full moon, neap tide. Those were the days."

After they said their good-byes, Ted sat for a long time pondering the matter of the disc. It seemed too much of a coincidence that his old pal Stan Thurlow was in possession of a disc from Xaviera Corporation. It was certainly too much to comprehend that the dead woman might be Gerald Toth's Xaviera, who had gone on to work for Ivor Beame. But if it turned out that the set of CDs Toth was sending him was missing disc number three of four, that would confirm something.

There was no further sign of any suspicious person driving along Timberhill Road that night, and the fog had not reappeared the next morning when Betty drove away to visit Sid Edwards at the nursing home upstate, not far from Hartford.

"He's been restless the past couple of days," the attendant told her when she arrived. "I guess he's been wondering where you were."

"I've had some business to take care of, Ellie, and I have to go to New York next week. I want to be sure that Mr. Edwards understands that I won't be visiting for two weeks, so I decided to explain it myself."

Sid had a nice room all to himself, which he could certainly afford, although the occasional short-term patient sometimes shared the room for a night or two while other arrangements were being made. He was lying motionless as always on the bed, his eyes closed. Betty thought he looked thinner and paler than she remembered from her visit the previous week.

"Sid," she whispered. "It's Betty." His eyes fluttered open, and although his face was incapable of registering emotion, she was certain he was trying to smile. He couldn't speak, although he did make some sounds now that he'd been having regular therapy.

"How are you feeling?" She knew it was a dumb question, but she understood him when he lowered his eyelids briefly. He was feeling okay, not great, but okay. The nursing-home attendants were always amazed that she seemed to understand what he was trying to say without actually speaking any words. "If you spend a long enough time with a person," she'd explained, "you get to know what he's thinking." They didn't believe her, but she did know that about Sid.

"I can't stay long," she said. "But I wanted to stop by to tell you that I have to go to New York on business next week, so it will be a while before I get back. Why? You remember me telling you about my neighbor Ted Kelso. He does work with computer programs and some big shot has offered him a lot of money to test a new program. Ted isn't sure he's trustworthy, so he wants me to go to the city to kind of interview him. Sort of the way I used to interview people for you." She watched Sid closely, then said, "He asked me because he trusts my judgment, but you're right. It is a bit odd. You remember I told you that Ted uses a wheelchair, so he doesn't want to go himself."

She knew that Sid was trying to speak, to ask her something. Then she saw a tiny frown. "It's not dangerous, I promise." The frown disappeared. "Except, well, Ted said something about rumors that the program might be stolen."

Now Sid really was trying to make words. She leaned closer to him and listened. There! She was sure she heard the words "cornered thief, victim, revenge."

"Don't tire yourself," she said. "I understand. You want me to be careful, because both the thief and the person he stole from are dangerous. Well, I suppose you're right. I understand quite a bit of potential money is involved."

Sid's therapy had enabled him to use his arms a bit and now he made a weak gesture as if pointing to his eyes.

"I understand. The truth will be in the man's eyes, no matter what comes out of his mouth. I've always relied on that, anyhow."

"Maa . . . Maas . . ." Sid said.

"Maa? Aha, Masters! Of course!" She'd guessed a name they both knew. Gavin Masters had worked for Edwards & Son for years, regularly removing pages of checks from the back of the checkbook, forging a signature, and arranging to have a coconspirator at a local bank cash them. It had worked for a time until their old bookkeeper uncovered the theft. Masters had denied everything when confronted by Betty and Sid, but they had both seen the guilt in his eyes. But that hadn't been all. Once they had cornered him, he had responded with violence, picking up a lamp on his desk and attempting to smash both Betty and Sid with it. A cornered thief. The office boy had come to their aid and Masters had been taken away, but Betty knew what Sid was trying to tell her now. She might quickly determine that the computer man was a thief, but if he knew that she knew, he was likely to react the same way that Masters had.

"I promise I'll be careful," Betty said. "He'll know pretty quickly that I don't know a thing about computer software, so I couldn't tell if something had been stolen. Besides, I'm a little old lady now. Surely important businessmen don't attack little old ladies on innocent errands."

Sid watched her wistfully.

"I promise I'll call Ellie every day to tell her I'm okay and she can tell you." His pale, thin hands tried to grasp the sheet covering his body. "Please, Sid, it won't do you any good to worry. Relax and do your therapy. I'll come back to you safe and sound, I promise." She touched his hand and then held it tightly until she felt him relax and drop into a doze. She watched him for a while, but he had fallen deeply asleep. She carefully removed her hand from his, touched his forehead gently, and then quietly left the room.

She found Ellie, the attendant, outside another patient's door. "I'm going to call you every day while I'm away so that you can reassure Mr. Edwards that I'm all right."

"Why wouldn't you be?"

"He's worried that the business I'm going away to handle is dangerous."

"Miss Trenka, no matter if you called me to say you were dead, I'll tell him you're as fine as the rosy dawn. No way would I tell that poor old man something happened to you. That would finish him for sure."

Betty left Penny Saks's number with Ellie, in case of emergency, and drove back to East Moulton, feeling somewhere between sad and elated. She was so sorry that Sid was ill and helpless, but no one had ever needed her as much as he did. For all her lack of purpose in life these days, Sid was still the only purpose she needed.

Well, Tina seemed to think she needed Betty. She was sitting in the kitchen near the food bowl, glaring angrily at its emptiness when Betty got home, but Betty was feeling charitable, so she chose to offer one of the expensive kitty gourmet cans instead of the usual economy-priced cat food Tina usually got. Tina had Sid Edwards to thank for this small blessing.

Betty devoted her evening to looking up Xaviera Corporation on the Internet, reading about its executives, reviewing its list of products, none of which meant anything to her. Gerald Toth's smiling, handsome face filled the screen, but there was no way she could read anything in his eyes.

CHAPTER 8

MARGARET COULDN'T decide whether she was truly looking forward to her Saturday dinner date with Gerald or whether she was merely curious to see how she would react to him after all this time. However, she had decided not to mention the dinner to De Vere and indeed had simply said that she was seeing some out-of-town friends when he rang her to see if she was free on Saturday evening.

Gerald was certain to take her to a fashionable, expensive restaurant, so she was determined to look her best. While she was pondering her wardrobe, she made arrangements with Poppy to obtain tickets for a cocktail reception the following week for one of the myriad charities that attracted social New York night after night.

"The usual people one sees all the time," said Poppy, who seldom actually saw anyone. "But they're polite enough and won't trouble themselves too much about who your friend might be. These charities are always seeking funds and high-profile people."

"Miss Trenka has no profile to speak of," Margaret said, "but one hopes she will enjoy mingling with the upper classes while clutching a glass of inferior white wine or even more inferior champagne. And you're right. Even the most offensive members of New York society are usually polite to little old ladies, who might well be the mother of somebody important and the hand that controls immense trust funds, and thus more charity dollars."

She decided on a classic little black dress for her dinner with Gerald, a pair of obscenely high stiletto heels—would that fashion never end?—and her late mother's emerald earrings, which looked especially nice with her blond hair and perfect English complexion. Her recent manicure would need repairs, so she made a Saturday-morning appointment. By doing so, she might well miss the ugly gossip that tended to swirl about Philip's salon. The majority of the most dedicated destroyers of reputations had their nails done earlier in the week, to be ready for Friday-night events.

Gerald, meanwhile, had managed to elicit assurances that a table would be found for him at the trendiest restaurant of the moment at around eight o'clock, in spite of the restaurant's policy against taking reservations. He even went so far as to commit himself and Margaret to the chef's justly renowned leg of lamb and flageolets, with lemon curd tart for dessert. Then he planned on taking her to one of the clubs on the West Side, where they could put in an appearance, even if Margaret didn't wish to linger. Then, perhaps, a nightcap at another fashionable spot frequented by bold-faced names. Even if he didn't come face-to-face with Brunetta, people would see him and Margaret together and word would filter back to her, he was sure of it.

The only decision he had to make was whether to take Sonny the bodyguard with them. Since he didn't keep a car in New York, he generally hired a limo when he needed one. The drivers were good but weren't necessarily trained to defend their passengers against danger. He doubted that Ivor Beame would attempt something nasty in a public place and he certainly didn't wish to have the imposing Sonny sharing his table with Margaret at dinner. Such a thing would definitely look peculiar to Brunetta, who might not be able to count to a hundred but did know how matters were handled in New York. Still, Sonny waiting in the limo or lurking outside on the street might be a good idea.

Sonny had been hanging around the apartment since Gerald summoned him, but he didn't intrude. Rather, he seemed fascinated by daytime talk shows and evening game shows. Gerald had heard him muttering answers to the questions posed to contestants, with occasional shouts of "You dummy. Everybody knows that." He could probably beat Brunetta easily at *Jeopardy!,* his biggest drawback being that he wasn't beautiful and Brunetta was.

So he asked Sonny if he'd mind doing guard duty

while his temporary boss dined out on Saturday. Sonny shrugged. "I do whatever I'm paid to do. I kinda like to get a look at the place ahead of time, though, so I know what I'm dealing with."

"I'll see that you do," Gerald said. "It's a new restaurant over on Ninth Avenue, but a ways down-town. A lot of the beautiful people go there."

"Then nobody's goin' to try to whack you there." Unspoken were the words "because they might hit somebody really important." Sonny shrugged again. "What do you say I just hang out with the car while you're inside? Keep an eye on who goes in and comes out. You know."

"Deal," Gerald said. He didn't mind using Margaret to further other aspects of his personal life, but he liked her and didn't want her to come to harm just because she was with him.

He ordered a car to pick Margaret up at her building and take her to the restaurant, then he took a taxi to Ninth Avenue in advance with Sonny beside him, to be sure he threw enough weight around to secure a good table and to give Sonny a chance to look the place over. He could tell that Sonny wasn't impressed by the restaurant or its location close to the meat-packing district. It was a plain, almost grubby place on the ground floor of an old brick building, with red doors and uninspired signage. Inside, there were faded, distressed mirrors, round white globes hanging from a high ceiling, plain tables. Sonny would probably have preferred the fancied-up Russian Tea Room, especially with the acrylic bear with fish swimming around inside, or, more likely, one of the many serious steakhouses that dotted the city. Big meat for big guys.

Of course, Gerald was ushered into the restaurant without hesitation in spite of the gaggle of desperate trendoids begging for a seat and a crust of bread.

Margaret arrived on time, looking serenely aristo-cratic in her simple black dress, spiced up with some very good jewelry. They brushed cheeks, not quite a kiss. Gerald noticed that people were covertly check-ing them out. He was rather well known, and a lot of people knew Lady Margaret. In return he recognized some other well-known faces from the worlds of en-tertainment, sports, and society. No Brunetta. He knew from experience that she didn't much care for food, preferring to sustain herself on cigarettes, vari-ous forms of caffeine, and, sometimes, quite a lot of controlled substances.

There was an awkward pause while they waited as the wine was served. Then Gerald said, "I wonder why it didn't work out between you and me."

"I was becoming a bit battered by all the social business, and Dianne Stark's tragedy was the final straw. I became quite incapable of sustaining a rela-tionship."

"We could have made a go of it," Gerald said.

Margaret sipped her wine and thought of De Vere.

Difficult though he was, he was sure and comfortable, although she still wasn't certain that a happy resolution for them lay ahead.

The waiter took their order.

"With you out of the picture, I started looking for . . ." He hesitated. "That's not entirely true. There was someone I cared for a good deal, and it was because she left me that I found myself attracted to you. Then with you gone, I decided that intelligent, accomplished women were wrong for me, so I started pursuing beautiful creatures who didn't waste much time being intelligent. I find that if one has enough money, it's fairly easy to find what one is looking for."

The food arrived and was delicious. Margaret did enjoy eating.

"I never thought I'd manage to get in here," she said, not wanting to discuss Gerald's quest for female companionship. The restaurant seemed a neutral topic. "I'm not so well known and I don't hang out at places like Balthazar. I don't hang out much at all anywhere, if truth be told. Of course, if I make a reservation someplace as Lady Margaret, people tend to find a spot for me, but I understood that one couldn't make reservations for this place."

"Ah, but I am well known," Gerald said, "and I do know the right people." He shrugged. "Things usually work out for me." Then he talked about things that had worked out for him. Very grand business successes, a hint of a business disaster. Nothing personal now, except for a brief and almost sad mention again of the woman who had left him and was somehow involved in the business disaster. Suddenly, he tossed a pale blue Tiffany box tied with a white ribbon on the table.

"A little something to commemorate our reunion." The temp, Gladys, had selected a small gold brooch with a lovely ruby in its center. Not only did Gladys have excellent taste, she was a fast typist. Plenty of good qualities, but alas, she was not beautiful and she had a grating Brooklyn accent.

"Mmm," Margaret said dubiously. She looked at the box and then at Gerald.

"I'm not trying to seduce you with expensive presents," he said. "I just wanted to give you something, and it happens that my secretary is devoted to shopping. So it wasn't even personally chosen by me. Will you accept it?"

Margaret grinned. "I might. Depends on what it is." She opened the box and sighed. "Lovely. I like rubies as much as emeralds. I accept, if you're sure you can afford it. I understand the upkeep of supermodels is extremely high."

He laughed. "Money is the least of my worries, and models come and go, since they migrate according to the demands of the fashion industry, which is responsible for their upkeep."

Margaret finished off her lemon curd tart. "I saw you talking to a rather large person when I arrived."

Gerald waved his hand. "It's just Sonny. My rent-a-bodyguard of the moment."

"Goodness! A bodyguard?"

"People have directed some unpleasant sentiments toward me recently. Threats, actually. I thought it would be wise to bring some protection. Sonny is a good fellow, very well trained and big. Fast thinker. Just what one wants in the way of a bodyguard."

But Margaret didn't seem to be listening. She was gazing across the room at a table of merry diners, one of whom stood up and seemed to be glaring at her. "Gerald, I do hope the unpleasant sentiments didn't come from a woman, because there's one over there who completely expresses the idea 'If looks could kill.' I think I know her, or at least recognize her. Isn't she . . ."

Gerald swiveled around and followed the direction of Margaret's gaze. Ah, bliss. It was the beautiful Brunetta, right on cue, shooting daggers in their direction. "Yes, I know her. Her name is Brunetta, and we used to go about together for a time. But I don't know what she has to be so angry about. She dumped me in no uncertain terms."

"Your Brunetta is very lovely." She didn't mention that the supermodel appeared to be slightly malnourished. "I'd hate to think she was busily plotting mischief. I wonder what she's thinking."

"Don't worry about that," Gerald said. "Thinking

is not her strong suit. Let's go somewhere and dance or listen to music."

"But not to one of those places where people shoot off guns in the crowd and it makes the front page of every paper in town."

"Certainly not," Gerald said. "Let's go."

They made their way out, avoiding Brunetta, and then through the crowd standing outside, still hoping to be admitted to the culinary sanctuary. Gerald introduced Margaret to Sonny, who looked her over approvingly. Margaret seemed to inspire sudden affection in persons who were, in the end, thugs. It had happened before, and it looked to be happening again. Sonny hastened to open the door of the limo for her, then settled his bulk in the front seat with the driver. He left Gerald to walk around the car to open his own door.

Suddenly, there was a commotion in the crowd outside the restaurant and a slim, blond woman—it could only be Brunetta, unwilling to give up easily—rushed toward the limo. She fumbled with her ridiculously small handbag and managed to extract an equally ridiculously tiny handgun, which she seemed to be aiming at Gerald, who ducked into the car. Sonny leaped out of the front seat in an instant and tackled her while the driver stepped on the gas and sped away.

"I hope he didn't damage her," Margaret said, straining to look out the back window. "He's rather large and she's very small."

Gerald wiped his brow and sighed. "At least she didn't manage to damage me, although that was clearly her intention. I would have thought, though, that she'd aim at you, since you have captured my attention, leaving her holding only her million-dollar modeling contract. I believe she had her sights set on my assets."

"But you said she broke it off with you."

"Probably just a ploy to sustain my interest."

"I wonder," Margaret said, "if she considers waving a weapon in your direction just another ploy to attract your interest."

"I wish she hadn't done that," Gerald said. "I have enough to worry about. Margaret, would you mind if we didn't go to clubland, just went somewhere quiet for a drink?"

"Not at all. But shouldn't we go back to the restaurant and see if we can extricate your burly friend from any difficulties he may find himself in?"

"I think Sonny can handle himself without assistance from us. If the police are called, there are plenty of witnesses to testify that the woman was waving a gun and Sonny was merely protecting me." He looked at her ruefully. "But I'll bet I won't get preferred treatment the next time I attempt to get a table there. Well, there are thousands of restaurants in Manhattan. I just hope my reputation doesn't precede me."

He had the driver take them to a quiet neighborhood place on the East Side, an Irish pub with a few regulars at the bar watching a sports event on the big-screen TV with the sound muted and two couples huddling over mugs of beer in the corners. Before leaving the car, he told the driver to tell Sonny where they were in case he called the car's cell phone. Then he reminded the driver to be alert for suspicious persons entering the pub.

"What kind of suspicious?"

"Anybody carrying a bazooka," Gerald said. "You'll know if you see them."

"You're really worried," Margaret said when they'd settled at a table. Their waitress had an Irish brogue and conveyed some hostility when she heard Margaret's English accent. Some issues will never die, no matter how long the politicians talk.

"Not worried so much as puzzled. I haven't done anything terrible to anyone except for what may have arranged itself in poor Brunetta's soft brain. She's so damned unpredictable, like a child who acts but hasn't thought things through. I made no commitment to her. Everybody dates models, drops one, takes up with another. Donald Trump is our role model, and nobody tries to shoot him for moving on. I have some business enemies, as does everyone who is successful. You have to do what you have to do to get ahead. But with very few exceptions, none of them would view my elimination as getting even. Far better to get even by being more successful and making more money."

But Margaret noticed that he shifted uneasily as

he spoke, his eyes scanned the room, and he became suddenly tense and alert as a couple of young guys came in from the street and joined their buddies at the bar.

"Ah, Gerald. Perhaps you'd be more comfortable if you were at home. And no, I'm not inviting myself to join you. Your driver can drop me off at my place and then you can go on to yours. If Sonny hasn't been arrested for forceful leaning on Brunetta, he's probably waiting for you at home."

"You're a perceptive woman, Margaret. Yes, I'll be able to relax away from a public place. I'll expect you to call me on Tuesday to say where I'll meet you and that woman for dinner. I'm not quite sure why she's here, but"—he shrugged—"that's the way Ted wanted to handle things. I hope she's not some kind of computer genius, because I'm certainly not. I just know what sells, and I'd hate to be shown up by a doddering old lady. After we have our get-acquainted meal, I'll see her the next day for whatever discussions she has in mind. Then I suppose I'll have to entertain her."

"Not to worry. I'm taking her to a charity reception on Wednesday, and I'll find out if she wants theater tickets or something for the rest of her visit. I don't imagine there's a lot to do in a small Connecticut town, and she's probably thrilled to be visiting New York. You're off the hook." Margaret tried her most winning smile. "Except . . . oh, I don't like to ask this, but if Miss Trenka wants to do a bit of sight-seeing, it might be hard for her to get around on foot and by public transportation . . ."

"You'd like to borrow a car. Done."

"I'll look after her. I promised Carolyn Sue."

CHAPTER 9

BETTY SPENT the weekend carefully packing for her trip to New York, with a brief time-out to discuss her assignment with Ted.

"I've read everything I could find about Xaviera Corporation," she told him, "and looked up some news stories about Gerald Toth. Just from reading them I judge him to be a typically astute businessman who made a great deal of money with that IPO a couple of years ago. He likes to call his company a software leader in a variety of fields. Business, the health-care industry, libraries and educational institutions, even prisons. I also judge that he's a different sort of fish from Bill Gates because he doesn't seem to want to own the world, just his selected corners of it. I suppose that means he's highly focused, possibly ruthless. Oh, and he doesn't seem to hesitate to use other people's developments. He uses Windows and sometimes UNIX. I'm beginning to sound like I know what I'm talking about. Which I don't."

She put down the sheaf of papers she'd brought with her into Ted's living room and sighed.

"You'll do just fine," Ted said. "You're a fast learner."

"I'm scared to death," Betty said. "Toth is going to know I don't know anything about his business."

"I've told you, you don't need to talk in technical terms. Besides, I'm pretty sure he's not a technical genius. He knows how to pick the right people to do the work. Look, all you have to do is get him to clarify what tasks he wants me to accomplish. Take notes, get a sort of timetable, set up benchmarks for what needs to be done. Since you're not supposed to know that there's anything fishy about the system I'm testing, you don't have to ask questions about it. Besides, he's denied that the program was pirated. You're posing as my assistant, remember, and assistants assist, organize, you know all about that."

She nodded, then told him about her visit to see Sid. "He looks so frail, as though he's barely clinging to life. But I told him about my job for you and he reminded me of a situation other than the one I mentioned to you, where I had to figure out what a prospective employee was really like behind a superb résumé."

"You'll do just fine," Ted repeated. Then he explained more about Enterprise Resource Management systems and gave her a list of the various projects he'd been associated with. "Toth knows all this, but he might try quizzing you, to see how knowledgeable you are about what I do. All of the assignments were completed to everyone's satisfaction; I found a few bugs in some of the software that I helped the developers correct. I don't think you need to know precisely which ones. You can say we're operating under nondisclosure agreements in all cases. He'll respect and accept that."

"That's it?" Betty had counted on Ted giving her more instructions.

"There's just one other puzzling matter. That dead girl on the beach was named Xaviera. I have a feeling that she could be the woman Toth named his company for. She had a vague connection with another company that deals in computers, Ivor Enterprises. In fact, this program I'm looking at is rumored to have been developed by Ivor Enterprises and then stolen, somehow ending up in Toth's hands. I wonder if she had anything to do with the theft. A friend of mine from my childhood at Redding's Point called me the other day and it appears he found a computer disc that seems to be from the Xaviera Corporation. His kids actually found the body. There's more, but I think the less I tell you now, the better. I'm going to Redding's Point to pick up the disc after I drop you off in New Haven. I'll pick you up on Monday around ten. That will get you to New Haven in good time to catch the noon train to New York. You'll be in the city—at Grand Central Station—shortly after one-thirty. Then you're to call Toth in the afternoon and he'll take you to dinner as arranged."

"I don't know that I want to meet him socially on my own before our meeting."

"You could cancel. I doubt that losing a dinner companion would bother him. Toth will probably want to meet with you on Tuesday or Wednesday. Think you'll be able to amuse yourself? You can call Carolyn Sue Hoopes, who's at the hotel."

"I am having dinner with a Lady Margaret Priam on Tuesday. Apparently she's a friend of Mrs. Hoopes's, who is going to be away from the city. Lady Margaret kindly offered to look after me, so I do have one little engagement. I plan to see a show, perhaps, and get in some sight-seeing. I'll be fine. I'm looking forward to it. Penny will see to the cat, so you don't have to concern yourself with that tiresome chore." Then she asked shyly, "Do you know Lady Margaret well? She indicated that she'd gotten my number from you. I mean, a real lady and all."

"I knew some members of her family. I haven't ever met her. Ah, Elizabeth, I hope your Sid is all right," Ted said. "It must be hard . . ."

"It is," Betty said. "Especially since Sid Junior and the rest of the family don't visit often, and with Mary gone, he really only has me." She gathered up her things in preparation for returning home.

"Wait, Elizabeth, we've never discussed your compensation. Besides your travel and hotel expenses and incidentals, I'll pay you five hundred dollars a day for your trouble."

Betty blinked. "Ted, that's far too much for so little effort on my part."

Ted smiled. "If I do my job for Toth properly and he pays me what he's dangled in front of me, it won't seem like much, and if you give me good reason not to work with him, it's a fair exchange."

"I won't have you paying me for the weekend," she said firmly. "That's my off time, and I see no reason to get paid for those two days."

"Okay, have it your way." The phone jangled softly and Ted wheeled himself over to answer it. Betty watched a frown spread and saw his jaw working, although he didn't say anything for a few minutes. Then he said coldly, "I don't know where you got your information, but I don't take kindly to threats, even implied ones." He listened again, then said, "Nothing you can say will change my mind about anything." He hung up abruptly and turned to face Betty.

"Some misinformed joker has just advised me not to get involved with Gerald Toth or I may live to regret it. I couldn't tell if it was a man or a woman. Elizabeth, I want you to be very careful. I don't think anybody other than Toth and perhaps Carolyn Sue and Lady Margaret know that you're acting as my representative, but if you notice anything or anyone suspicious, move yourself into a situation where there are a lot of people and look for protection—a policeman, a security guard. There's safety in numbers or in crowds."

"I'll be very careful, and you should do the same."

"I'm always careful, and nobody's going to bother me," he said. But he still looked concerned, and he didn't mention the car that had driven by slowly the other night, inspecting the mailboxes as if searching for his.

Betty stepped out into the brisk night. The weather had turned clear and fine, and the black sky was littered with tiny points of starlight. She gazed upward after she crossed Timberhill Road and reached the path to her front door. There seemed to be more stars than usual, a veritable net of them covering the heavens. I should study astronomy, she thought, to recognize the constellations, and wondered if the stars in Rome, London, and Vienna looked the same as in this quiet corner of Connecticut. She'd find out in the spring.

She'd left the lights on in her house, so when she entered her brightly lit living room, she immediately saw the black pile of Tina curled up on the sofa. The cat sprang up at her entrance and grudgingly circled around Betty's legs as though to convey affection that Betty was certain didn't exist.

"You'll miss me when I'm away, my friend," Betty murmured.

She had nothing much to do until she departed for the train. She checked her list of tasks once more, but everything was done. As an afterthought, she decided to slip her passport into her handbag in case she needed a more official identification than a Connecticut driver's license, even though she was quite certain that she didn't need a passport to enter New York City.

She found it difficult to get to sleep that night. Her mind was racing, tumbling with thoughts about what lay ahead for her. She knew she could handle the Gerald Toth assignment, but she wondered what Lady Margaret would be like. Like today's modern nuns, titled ladies certainly didn't go about in their traditional regalia—tiaras and ermine robes and such. A pity.

Time passed quickly, and Monday arrived, and then it was ten o'clock. Her small suitcase was at the door, her nice black suede coat was on a chair, and she was rechecking her handbag when she saw Ted's car back out of his driveway, ease across the road, and stop in front of her house. Tina watched mistrustfully as Betty donned her coat and checked the kitchen door to make sure it was locked. She had to push Tina back from the front door with her foot when the cat decided it was time to go outdoors and slaughter field mice.

"If you were a dog, I'd say 'Sit, stay,'" Betty said. "But you're not and I won't. Can't go out now. The boys will let you out later."

She locked the front door and went to the car.

"Are you sure you have enough wining and dining clothes in that little bag?" Ted asked.

"Enough, and I've decided that if I need more clothing, there are plenty of shops in New York."

They drove along country roads until they reached the highway, then joined the stream of cars and huge trucks speeding south on the Connecticut turnpike. Ted reviewed some of the things they'd discussed about Xaviera Corporation and Gerald Toth, but there really wasn't much new to say. They glided off the turnpike onto a New Haven exit ramp, drove along some mean streets, then onto a broad avenue that brought them to the railroad station. Ted handed her money for her ticket and said, "Call me about anything, anytime. Advice, counsel, help. I'll be at my post as usual. Except that after I leave you, I'm driving up the coast to Redding's Point. Good luck." Then Betty was on her own. Ted wondered if he should have told her more about the disc, about his suspicion that it had come from the ERP program, that Xaviera had gone on to work for Ivor Beame.

The New Haven station had a high soaring ceiling, with rows of wooden benches in the middle, where a number of well-dressed matrons chatted while they waited for the train to New York. Betty went to the row of windows along the wall and purchased a round-trip ticket to Manhattan.

"Next New York train is on track five," the ticket seller said. "Go down those steps, along the passageway until you see the sign for the track, then up the stairs to the platform. The train should be ready for boarding in about fifteen minutes. Don't take the Boston Amtrak train, which will be arriving in five minutes on track seven. They won't honor your ticket and it will take you to Penn Station rather than to Grand Central."

"Thanks," Betty said, then watched the words and numbers flip over quietly on the overhead arrivals and departures sign. The train from Boston was three minutes away. She decided to go to her platform to breathe some fresh air before she boarded the train. As she reached track five, she saw the long silver train from Boston glide into the station two tracks away.

Businesspeople, along with what were clearly Yale students and a crowd of others, got off the train and hurried down the steps that led into the station. Then an empty train eased into place on track five. The doors slid open and the people waiting for the local to New York entered. Betty picked a car in the middle of the train and found a window seat near the end of the car. She was on the left-hand side of the car, which she calculated would give her a view of Long Island Sound as the train traveled west to New York. But she wouldn't glimpse the beach where that young woman died. Redding's Point was to the east, at the other end of the state's coastline.

She wished she'd thought to buy some coffee in the station, as others around her appeared to have done, but it wasn't a long trip to New York and she'd find some lunch when she arrived. This midday train wasn't crowded, and nobody took the seat beside her. The train pulled out of the station and they were on their way to Bridgeport, Norwalk. Stamford. She saw the signs for Darien, Cos Cob, Green's Farms, and Westport flash by. There were glimpses of Long Island Sound, of elegant houses and tree-shaded streets. Soon, when they reached the outskirts of New York, the scene changed into a landscape of grubby, ramshackle factories, warehouses, and apartment buildings. Glimpses of streets with piles of debris in the gutters and graffiti painted on the brick walls. Abandoned cars and clusters of children playing in the streets. The train stopped at 125th Street in Harlem, and she noticed many more black faces among the passengers waiting on the platform. A few more minutes and the train plunged into a tunnel so dark, she couldn't see the walls, although feeble lights shed a pale glow as the train sped past.

"Last stop Grand Central in three minutes," the disembodied voice of the conductor said over the loudspeaker. The other passengers began to gather up their belongings, tossing their newspapers aside and dropping their empty coffee containers on the floor. When the train came to a stop at a bare platform at the end of the tunnel, Betty picked up the suitcase at her feet and followed the others to the exit. She stepped out onto the platform and joined the exodus heading toward the archway beyond the engine.

Suddenly she was in the cavernous, beige Grand

Central Terminal, facing a row of shops that looked brand new. She remembered reading in the *New York Times* that the station had recently been renovated to restore it to its former grandeur. To her right, she could see the vast main room and even caught a glimpse of the deep blue ceiling high above it, decorated in gold and little lights representing all the constellations. To her left, a broad passageway seemed to lead to the street, where she hoped to find a taxi. She looked up and admired the Diego Rivera mural covering the ceiling of the passageway.

She got into the first hovering taxi she encountered on busy Lexington Avenue. "Villa d'Este hotel," she said, and gave the East Side address. The driver, who wore a turban and a thick beard, said nothing and turned on the meter. He quickly brought her to a quiet, tree-lined street and stopped in front of a small brownstone building. It didn't look like any hotel she'd ever seen, but there on the awning, in discreet white letters, were the words "Villa d'Este." A uniformed doorman stood proudly at the door. Then she noticed that the hotel had spread to the adjoining brownstones, so it wasn't as small as it appeared at first viewing.

Inside, the lobby was elegant, even lavish. There was a small lounge area, with tall ferns and potted palms offering some seclusion for the tables and comfortable armchairs, where even in the early afternoon a few people were enjoying cocktails and glasses of wine. Toward the back she saw a restaurant, with mirrors that reflected the crisp white table-cloths and crystal stemware.

The young man at the registration desk did not seem impressed by her appearance. "May I help you, madam?"

"Yes, please. Elizabeth Trenka. I have a reservation." The desk clerk appeared to doubt her, then said, "Ah, yes. Miss Trenka. Aha!" He gave her an almost fawning look. "You have a message from Mrs. Hoopes." He handed her an envelope. A message from his boss did impress him, Betty decided, even if her black suede coat didn't.

"Thank you so much." She glanced at the note. Carolyn Sue was away at a spa but hoped to be back in time to see her. "I'm so sorry to have missed Mrs. Hoopes."

"Mrs. Hoopes is expected back next week, perhaps by the weekend," the clerk said. "A lovely woman. And the owner of this hotel."

"So I understand. A lovely woman," Betty said mendaciously.

"I'll have someone take your bags to your room."

"I've only the one," Betty said. "I can—"

But she was being handed a cardkey to her room, and someone had lifted her bag and was waiting for her. Betty followed the bellhop to a tiny elevator, and they rode to the fifth floor.

"We hope you'll find this room comfortable. If you need anything, directions or other assistance, please call the concierge. Here's the air conditioning, the heat. There is an ice machine just around the corner. The restaurant is open for breakfast, lunch, and dinner, and room service is available twenty-four hours a day. We serve a nice English tea every day at four. Enjoy your stay at the Villa d'Este."

He had been so solicitous that she gave him two dollars, although she imagined most guests gave him far more. He appeared to be satisfied.

Betty unpacked her few clothes and hung them in the closet, where she found an iron and an ironing board. If she was lucky, the wrinkles in her green satin jacket and lovely new long black dress would shake out and she wouldn't be forced to do a chore she avoided at home. But, of course, as the friend of Carolyn Sue Hoopes, she could probably demand that someone come and take her garments away for pressing, and it would be done immediately.

She peeked out the window. Her room faced the street, so she could watch the car and foot traffic if all else failed. She noticed a coffee shop on the corner across the street and decided to venture out for something to eat. She didn't feel like sitting in an empty hotel dining room, munching on a club sandwich, while the bored waiters wished she would go away.

There was a television set in an armoire facing the huge bed with piles of pillows and a bathroom loaded with hand cream, shampoo, soap, sewing kit, and more towels than she imagined any one person needed. Then she noticed the flower arrangement on a table in the corner. The card read "Welcome to New York," and it was signed "Gerald Toth." The basket of fruit beside it was from Carolyn Sue herself. "So sorry to have missed you. Enjoy my little home." There was even a bottle of white wine half hidden behind the ice bucket "compliments of the Villa d'Este."

She was all set. Then the phone rang.

"Hullo, Miss Trenka? Margaret Priam here. I see you are here in good time. Any difficulties?"

"No, it was quite easy," Betty said. "I just now arrived."

"I'm afraid I'm engaged tonight or I would come round to see you. But I'll ring in the morning about dinner. Ah . . . Gerald Toth has agreed to join us, if that suits you."

She felt a clutch of nervousness. "No, I mean, yes, that will be fine."

"I know you were to have dinner with him tonight, but he and I decided to cancel his plans for you this evening. I hope you're not disappointed."

"Not at all," Betty said. "I'm a little tired out by my trip, so I'll get to bed early instead."

"You must be puzzled about me taking over your social activities, but I've known Gerald for some time, and when he mentioned he had business with you, I thought it might be an opportunity for you to get to know him in advance of serious talk. And you might like to have a third party present, so you don't get involved in business talk over dinner. I think instead of ringing you tomorrow, I'll come round to your hotel at about seven and we'll go on to the restaurant and meet Gerald there. He's offered us the use of his car."

"That will be fine," Betty said.

"Lovely! I'll see you tomorrow evening, but if there's anything I can do for you in the interim, please don't hesitate to ring me."

Betty hadn't had so many people eager to assist her in years, if ever.

She went down to the lobby, exited the hotel, crossed the street, and ate a rather good club sandwich at the corner coffee shop, and watched the comings and goings of New Yorkers on the street outside the window.

CHAPTER 10

A*FTER LUNCH,* Betty decided to finish the first day of her visit to New York by wandering slowly down Second Avenue until she spotted the glass slab of the United Nations building on the skyline to her left. She turned down Forty-fourth Street on her way to First Avenue, passing some fine old apartment buildings and a big glass hotel on the corner. A row of national flags of UN member countries flapped gently from tall flagpoles along the front of the building, while a herd of hulking tourist buses expelled a stream of eager Japanese sight-seers bedecked with cameras. They mounted the short flight of stairs and passed through the wrought-iron gate onto the broad plaza. They moved in an orderly pack toward the visitors' entrance. Betty followed them. Many couldn't resist stopping in front of an eye-catching piece of sculpture that depicted a huge revolver with its barrel twisted into a knot. They took turns being photographed in front of the massive granite block on which the gun rested.

Betty didn't know much about firearms, but she suspected that if the twisted barrel were straightened, the proportions would be such that it could not be fired, even if a few oversize football players were recruited to pull the trigger. It was rather like the monster ants and spiders depicted in horror films. If they were real, they would be crushed under their own weight, or their slim legs couldn't possibly support their huge bodies. Still, the Japanese tourists seemed to find the twisted gun concept appealing.

She wasn't really interested in touring the UN today, so she merely went inside to view the sterile 1950s white marble entrance hall, the pendulum hanging from a very high point in the ceiling, and the spectacular tapestry depicting magical-realism birds and beasts hanging above the security checkpoint. A leaflet informed her that it was a Foucault's pendulum, which offered proof of the rotation of the Earth, and that the tapestry had been made by women from a Latin American country. She didn't care to stand in line to pass through metal detectors to ensure that she wasn't carrying weapons or explosives, so she left the building and took a look around.

A broad green lawn stretched out toward a row of trees on a level below the plaza. It looked as though it should be filled with frolicking children, but when she walked toward the East River, down some steps, and stood under the branches of Japanese cherry trees, now resting up for the coming winter, she saw signs strongly forbidding trespass on the grass. The only creatures that seemed to be allowed to enjoy the lawn were the squirrels, who scurried through the grass. Tina would make short work of them.

She strolled along the esplanade above the river and watched a few tankers and cargo ships moving slowly upriver; admired the bridges spanning the river both up- and downstream; took a look at the fading blossoms in the rose garden; glanced at the unimpressive skyline across the river with a large Pepsi-Cola sign, a strange green monolith of a building, and the cluster of derelict buildings on a narrow island in midstream, which she later learned were hospital buildings where Typhoid Mary had once been housed. She couldn't help noticing the young man with a pipe who was leaning over the esplanade wall, apparently gazing down at a traffic jam on the FDR Drive below the UN complex. He was fairly nondescript, although it was unusual to see a young man smoking a pipe. Then she noticed him again as she walked to the end of the esplanade and visited the little nook with a bench dedicated to Eleanor Roosevelt.

She decided to go back to the hotel for a rest, and when she passed through the gates to the street, she looked back but didn't see the young man behind her.

She didn't feel entirely comfortable in the city yet. Cars, taxis, and buses roared up First Avenue. It was all too busy and confusing. The homeless man begging for spare change, pigeons eating an abandoned slice of pizza on the sidewalk, dark Africans in native dress with photo IDs on chains around their necks. UN personnel, no doubt, as were the Indian women in saris and even a man in an orange robe with a shaved head—a Tibetan monk, of all things. Nursemaids pushed carriages crammed with babies and toddlers. Shoppers entered and left supermarkets and shops. The bustle was very tiring.

She bought a diet soda and a cheese Danish at a deli, so she would have a snack for the evening, in case she didn't care to face either the starchy restaurant or a room-service waiter at the hotel.

She didn't notice the black town car with tinted windows breathing quiet fumes as it idled a few car lengths away from the hotel entrance. A polite young man in a hotel uniform stopped her as she approached the elevator.

"Miss Trenka? There was a message left to be handed to you personally."

"Me?" She said it before bothering to wonder how this dewy youth knew who she was. Perhaps it was the magic of association with Carolyn Sue Hoopes.

"A Mr. Ivor Beame was here to see you and left the message."

"A mistake, I'm sure," Betty said. "I don't know a Mr. Beame," but she had heard of him, so she took the envelope and read the message in the elevator.

It would profit you to meet with me
tomorrow at eleven in the morning. I will
send my car at ten. Ivor Beame.

It was a thoughtful Betty who carried the bag of
pop and Danish to her room. Ivor Beame was Gerald
Toth's competitor, according to Ted. But how could
he have known about her, where she was staying,
even that she was in New York?

I don't need this complication, she thought, but
knew that she would be ready to meet him when the
car arrived in the morning. At the ice machine, she
filled the bucket with lots of tiny cubes, then put on
her new flannel nightdress and her cozy pink robe,
poured the soda into a squat heavy glass with ice,
and selected a perfect blushing pear, exactly ripe
enough, from the fruit basket. She piled up the down-
filled pillows, dimmed the lights, and turned on the
television set to doze through an old black-and-white
movie. It was a pleasure to fall asleep without a cat
kneading the blankets or lying on her face.

She woke early and disoriented. This wasn't her
narrow bed in East Moulton. She heard sirens and
honking horns. She heard footsteps in the hall and
the rattle of crockery. The TV was still on, so she
found a news channel to learn what disasters had
taken place around the world while she slept. Nothing to speak of, and it was eight o'clock. Ivor Beame
would appear in two hours. Fortunately, she didn't
require a lot of time to pull herself together, but she

was wary of meeting the man. She knew nothing about him except for what Ted had told her. She hadn't checked on his background at all.

She treated herself to breakfast in the restaurant, which seemed less formal in the morning. It seemed expensive to her, but Ted had told her to charge everything to her room and he would take care of all her expenses. The more she thought about Ivor Beame, the more uneasy she became. Finally she left the restaurant and called Ted on his cell phone.

"I'm in the car," he said. "I've just left my friend Stan's house at Redding's Point. I won't tell you about it now. What's the problem?" He listened while she explained about Beame's message.

"I think you ought to see him," Ted said. "You can do the same inspection of him that I hired you to do of Gerald Toth. What's he like, what's he thinking. That sort of thing. Tell you what. If you're worried about meeting him alone, call your friend Lady Margaret and tell her that you're meeting with him, just so somebody other than me knows what you're doing. But I wouldn't worry, Elizabeth. You don't know anything about the system, where it came from, what it does. You don't even have to worry about not mentioning my name and my role in all this. I'm certain he already knows all about me and what Toth has asked me to do."

"Mmm, Miss . . . Lady Margaret? This is Elizabeth Trenka. I'm sorry to trouble you, but . . ."

"No trouble I'm sure, Miss Trenka. How can I help you?"

"I just spoke to my . . . employer, Ted Kelso, and he suggested I call you to say . . ." She wasn't sure how to go on. "It's just that a man associated with Gerald Toth, not necessarily a friend of his, has pretty much commanded me to meet with him at eleven. I'm not privy to the details of Mr. Toth's business, nor do I understand all the ramifications of Ted's business relationships, so I don't know why Ivor Beame would want to meet with me. Ted thought it would be wise to tell someone in the city what I was doing, just in case. . . . This must sound silly to you. I have no reason to mistrust Mr. Beame."

"I believe I know the name," Margaret said. "Another purveyor of computer things, like Gerald. Well, consider me informed, and if you aren't back by the time we're to meet for dinner, I will certainly sound the alarm. Gerald will know what to do."

Betty felt strangely relieved that Margaret knew, that Gerald Toth would know if necessary, and, of course, that Ted knew. She donned a sober tweed suit and pinned up her hair. In a matter of minutes she was ready to descend to the lobby to read a newspaper until Ivor Beame appeared at ten. She imagined he would be right on time.

As she was now widely recognized by the hotel staff as Carolyn Sue's friend, she was lavished with attention as she sat in a comfortable armchair under a palm tree. Someone brought her coffee unasked, another placed a pile of magazines and newspapers on the table beside her, and the nice young man who had given her Ivor Beame's message hovered unobtrusively in the distance, ready to fulfill any wish she might be about to voice. From where she sat, she could see the large decorative clock above the registration desk, so she watched the minutes tick by. Precisely at ten a man in a dark suit with his cap tucked under his arm entered the Villa d'Este, spoke to Betty's personal young man, and was escorted by him to her chair. She was certain this was not Ivor Beame himself.

"Miss Trenka, Dixon here will take you to your appointment. The car is just outside."

"Thank you so much. Would you be kind enough to accompany me to the car?" Another precaution. She didn't wish to be kidnapped with no one to witness it.

The young man glanced around nervously, as though leaving his post in the lobby was a serious offense. "Certainly, Miss Trenka." He took her arm and walked her through the revolving door.

"I assume that is the car," he said. The black town car with tinted windows was parked directly in front of the hotel, the doorman keeping watch for ticket-bestowing traffic agents. Suddenly, she saw the young man from the UN watching as the chauffeur opened the door of the town car and handed her in. There was no one else in the car. Well, of course an important man like Ivor Beame wouldn't appear in person.

He'd be waiting for her in his big Wall Street office, sitting behind an impressive desk, answering phone calls, and doing deals.

The darkened windows made it difficult for Betty to see where they were going, but soon enough they were on a high bridge crossing a span of silvery water. She could see in the distance the United Nations building, the Chrysler Building, and a stretch of highway along the river and realized that they were crossing the East River, which she'd walked beside only the day before. They weren't going into the heart of the Manhattan business district at all, but away from the city toward what she remembered from maps to be Long Island.

Betty rapped on the glass that separated her from the chauffeur. He pushed a button and the glass lowered enough for her to speak to him. "Where might we be going?"

"To Mr. Beame's place on the Island, ma'am," he said. "Those were my instructions. It won't take long, half an hour, forty-five minutes at the most, depending on traffic." The window was raised again, and Betty was left to try to calm her anxiety. Ivor Beame'd never said she'd be leaving the city; he'd never even told her what it was all about.

They drove through ordinary, drab neighborhoods with almost identical two-story brick houses with tiny front lawns, then onto a highway. They passed a big round sports stadium with a sign for Shea Stadium, the New York Mets' baseball park.

She glimpsed a tremendous globe showing the continents and remembered it was the site of a past World's Fair.

They passed La Guardia Airport, where she could see planes taking off and coming in for landings. Then the town car glided off the highway onto an ordinary two-lane road. Now they were passing through a residential area, where the houses weren't exactly identical but had a certain sameness as they crouched together with little land between them. Soon the houses were much grander and widely separated by lawns and landscaping. A very nice neighborhood. Gradually the houses were spaced farther and farther apart, tall, closed gates guarded driveways, and big old trees loomed up behind high concrete-and-brick walls. Nice and exclusive, at least in the owners' minds.

Finally the driver eased up to a closed gate and pushed a device on the dashboard; the gate swung open. They proceeded along a tree-lined drive to a rather imposing house with a Mediterranean look, complete with a row of tall cypress trees, stucco walls, red-tiled roof, and flower boxes crammed with fading geraniums and petunias. It seemed that they had arrived.

The driver opened the car door for Betty, and her feet crunched on the neatly raked, snowy pebbles of the drive. He gestured for her to go to the front door, then drove the car around the side of the house.

A rather plain maid in a gray uniform answered her

ring. "Elizabeth Trenka to see Mr. Beame," she said. The maid nodded and walked away across a broad foyer. Inside, the Mediterranean influence didn't seem as pronounced. It seemed a bit more Southwestern there. The floor was covered with waxed brownish-orange tiles, and the flower arrangements set on California mission–style wooden tables tended to dried branches and a few exotic flowers. The maid opened a door and gestured for Betty to enter. The room was definitely some decorator's idea of Southwestern: colorful woven Indian area rugs, a huge stone fireplace, cattle horns mounted on the walls, and comfortable puffy sofas and chairs in pale yellows and blues with throw pillows covered in black-and-white ponyskin. A black wrought-iron chandelier with real candles hung above it all.

"Mr. Beame will be down shortly, at eleven," the maid said, as though it was Betty's fault that she was fifteen minutes early. "Have a seat." She stopped at the door. "He's having one of his good days, so he shouldn't be long." Then she was gone.

One of his good days? That was the way Ellie at the nursing home talked about Sid. She had been imagining that Ivor Beame was a forceful, dynamic businessman with a grudge. Now she didn't know what to expect—a sick man, an aging tycoon? Ted hadn't said anything about him. She settled herself on a sofa and got out the mystery book she had started to pass the time. But it was a mere ten minutes before she heard the door open, then saw a bent, white-haired old man moving slowly while leaning on a walker. A young and remarkably beautiful woman assisted him. She was blond and unsmiling, and when she whispered something to him, he waved her away brusquely.

The young woman left, with a backward look at Betty, and Betty stood to meet Ivor Beame. Their eyes met briefly, then he looked away as though she were as inconsequential as an annoying housefly. He looked up at the dangling chandelier and gazed for a moment at the cow horns on his walls.

"Miss Elizabeth Trenka," he said. His voice was strong enough but raspy. "Formerly office manager of Edwards & Son, East Hartford, Connecticut. Retired. Presently a resident of East Moulton, Connecticut, lives alone. No permanent employment, takes odd jobs. Has been involved with a couple of murders." Did she detect a note of contempt in his voice?

She was surprised that he had searched out information about her and raised her hand to silence him. "I know who I am, where I live, and what I've done," she said. "The only thing you forgot to mention was my cat. Surely you didn't bring me here to discuss the joys of ordering copier paper and ballpoint pens for an office or finding a dead body dumped in my garage."

He nodded, then continued his slow progress toward a wing chair near the sofa she had chosen. She remained standing until he had maneuvered himself into his seat. "Sit down," he said gruffly. She sat on the edge of the sofa and waited to hear what he wanted of her.

"As you can no doubt see, Miss Trenka, I am an old man, somewhat disabled by the afflictions of age. I once had a charming and devoted wife of many years, and scattered about the country I still have two sons and a daughter, all of them dutifully producing fine grandchildren. I have spent my life building very solid businesses. Today my principal business involves computer software and such, because I saw and understood that these devices would change our world. So I got into the business early, and they did. Fifty years ago I was a programmer. Assembler." He had a faraway look in his eyes. "They don't use that language anymore, but I bet I could still do it and turn out a damned fine program, better than that crook Gerald Toth, who doesn't know a damned thing about software. Well, Miss Trenka, I got away from the hands-on stuff by hiring the best people to do the grunt work for me and I concentrated on building up the company. I kept away from the hardware side, decided to let IBM and those fellows worry about the machines while I worried about how to make them work."

He leaned back in his chair and Betty wondered if he was dozing off, but he said, "I was at it before Bill Gates was walking on two legs. I was determined to leave my kids and grandkids a pile of wealth, and I nearly made it a few years back, but I did something foolish. I hired a sharp young guy named Elliott

Wolfson, a real hotshot programmer who was twice as good as I ever was. Elliott was like a son to me almost, and he wasn't just someone who loved computers, he had a real business sense. I thought he'd take over from me when I retired. My boys wouldn't know how to run a company if their next glass of Merlot or round of golf depended on it. I suppose I spoiled them. I know I did, but I had Elliott. Then I didn't. He suddenly resigned and went off to work for Gerald Toth at Xaviera Corporation. Toth and I had been competitors for years, so Elliott's defection hit me hard, but you got to expect that sort of thing in business. His ingratitude almost killed me. Loyalty isn't a big issue nowadays."

Ivor Beame looked immeasurably sad, as though he never expected that sort of thing at all and loyalty was actually a very big issue with him. Betty felt a bit sorry for him, but she was wary. She still didn't know why she was there.

"The cruelest blow of all, Miss Trenka, was that when Elliott left me, he took with him a highly valuable product, one that would have brought in millions of dollars and allowed my boys to buy their own damned golf courses and just about anything else they or their sister and the grandkids wanted. Elliott was swayed by a woman, of course. He did it so that he could afford to buy the affection of a silly woman. Not that you'd think of Elliott as a ladies' man to look at him. I know the woman—she later worked for me for a time—and she wouldn't have looked twice at Elliott if there hadn't been the promise of money. I believe she was his accomplice in stealing my property—work he'd done for me, and it was mine. He offered it to Toth, who accepted it without hesitation. Or maybe the woman was the go-between. Gerry likes a beautiful woman as much if not more than the next man. She might even have known him before." Beame seemed quite agitated, and Betty wondered if she should call someone. "It's a very serious business, Miss Trenka. Are you sure you want to be involved in a theft, especially one of this magnitude?"

"Well, of course, theft is serious whatever its magnitude," Betty said cautiously, not certain what response he wanted or even where this conversation was heading.

"It was worse than theft," Beame said heatedly. "It was an attempt to murder me, to kill me off. He knows my heart is bad, everyone does. And if I was dead, who would know for sure that Elliott had taken the program and turned it over to my chief rival, Gerald Toth? Who would make Toth answer for his crime? Toth knew he was receiving stolen property, but he didn't return the program. In fact, he denied everything."

"Surely someone at your company besides you knew about the program. I mean, if someone was developing a major program, his colleagues must have had some idea. So even if you were dead—which I see you are not—someone could still have brought up the matter of theft. I understand software development is very expensive, so your accounting people would have records that show what your employee Elliott was working on, what he was getting paid for. And I should imagine," she said carefully, "that evidence must also exist on computer hard drives at your company." Now she was on shakier ground. She could readily understand employee theft of a valuable asset and solid filing cabinets filled with paper documents showing what work was in progress, but she wasn't entirely clear about whether someone like Elliott Wolfson could readily delete incriminating evidence from a computer hard drive. She understood that it wasn't all that easy to wipe a computer's memory totally clean.

"I really am sorry to hear that you were betrayed by a favored employee, Mr. Beame, but I do wish you'd get to the reason I'm here."

He gazed at her for a moment, and she could see in him something of Sid with his pale skin and thin hands. His speech, however, was perfectly clear, and except for the walker he used to get around, she saw no other signs of the heart condition he mentioned.

Then she tried to imagine how Sid would have felt if she or another trusted employee had robbed him of his most valuable project.

He would have been devastated, but more because of the betrayal of trust than the loss of money.

"You're here, dear lady, because you work for a person who will enable Gerald Toth to get away with his crime." Betty blinked at his vehemence and said nothing. "I know that Gerald is going to have my software—*mine*—tested by your employer. He's well respected, and if he says everything is on the up-and-up, people will believe him. Nobody will want to believe he's lying to cover up the theft.

"Now I don't believe you can persuade him to refuse to do the testing. Toth has probably offered him a lot of money. Nor can you convince him to announce that he's determined the program was pirated, although he surely knows it was without looking at it. I've heard the rumors flying everywhere. But perhaps you can persuade him that he is risking his well-being by becoming involved with this business—and to make you more amenable to trying to, let me say that I have quite a bit of money myself and will make it worth your while to work for my side. Very much worth your while. And if you choose not to ally yourself with me, I . . . I could make existence quite difficult for you."

Betty didn't care for the threatening undertone of his words. She stood. "Mr. Beame, you indicated that loyalty was a lost commodity, but I, for one, have not lost it, and I have committed myself to the person who hired me. I don't wish to entertain your proposal. May I please be returned to New York City?"

He waved his hand feebly. "I am an old man, Miss Trenka, and my health is not good. I don't expect I'll survive much longer, and I don't know that I care to. I still have a few friends, but even she . . . they are friends because they think they will profit from being so. It's easy to fool an old man into a marriage, for example, and make him think it's being done for love."

How could she have imagined he was like Sid, who wouldn't survive much longer himself, yet kept hanging on, because he understood that he was loved?

"But I do want to be sure that what is mine is returned to me," Ivor Beame continued. "Your so-called employer is making himself a party to a crime and is putting your life as well as his own in danger."

Elizabeth Trenka was not a fearful person, but she was suddenly afraid of Ivor Beame. On the other hand, she was not one to listen to threats without answering.

"Mr. Beame, you insult my intelligence. You can be sure that if any harm comes to me or Ted Kelso, we will have left evidence pointing directly to you. I certainly didn't come here in secrecy. My whereabouts are known."

She stood, turned on her heel, and left the room.

Behind her, she could hear Ivor Beame chuckling. Then she heard him shout, "Get that pretty little bag of skin and bones in here! And you, Miss Trenka, don't leave. I have more to say to you."

She didn't heed him but went out to the hallway.

"I'll call you before you return to Connecticut. You might have a change of heart."

CHAPTER 11

THE MAID bustled from the back of the house to open the door for Betty. That was when she noticed the slim, blond woman who had assisted Ivor Beame earlier. The woman scooted out of one room and quickly crossed the foyer to duck into another. Possibly she was his daughter or granddaughter. In any case, she had probably been eavesdropping on their conversation; she also seemed intent on not being noticed.

The maid hastened to open the door for Betty, who said, "I suppose that was one of Mr. Beame's granddaughters. She seems devoted to him. It's unusual to see a young woman caring for an elderly man."

"Those kids of his wouldn't be caught dead in this house with him, unless he's handing out birthday checks. That was nobody." Betty heard the contempt in the maid's voice. "Devoted, maybe. Devoted to money and what's good for herself. 'My caregiver,' he calls her. Whatever kind of care Her Majesty Miss

Bunny Trouble knows how to give. But I've told the
old man that if he marries her like he threatens to do,
I'm gone in an hour, and so are the rest of the servants." She stopped talking abruptly. "I shouldn't be
gossiping. I'd better see to the old man, since Miss
Trouble doesn't seem to feel like doing any 'caregiving' today." The maid quickly went to the room in
which Betty had met with Ivor Beame. Bunny Trouble? What sort of name was that?

She stepped outside and took a look around at the
lushly landscaped grounds. A few trees were starting
to turn, but the sky was blue and the sun was warm.
The car was at the door, ready to depart. Betty hesitated, then went back into the house. The car could
wait for a few minutes. She went to the room into
which the young woman had disappeared. It was another sitting room, much less aggressively Southwestern in decor. Miss Trouble was sitting in a chair,
presumably reading, but Betty noticed that the book
was upside down, and it was a dictionary to boot.
Not exactly light reading.

"Hello," Betty said. "I'm Elizabeth Trenka. I noticed you assisting Mr. Beame and I wondered . . ."

"I'm not allowed to talk about him," the woman
said. "He says I always get the facts wrong anyhow,
so you can wonder all you like. I have nothing to say
to you."

"I was merely concerned about his health."

"He's got no health. All that money and no health.
That's a real riot. What he needs is someone to pro-

tect him from his awful kids and the creeps who work for him, or used to work for him."

"Sounds like what he needs is a wife," Betty said. She noticed that the woman hadn't bothered to introduce herself, so she wasn't going to find out if her name really was Trouble.

"Yeah, that's what he needs. I just hope he doesn't pop off before he decides to get one. Never mind, I've got him where I want him. It's only a matter of time. And if that doesn't work out, I have, what do you call it, a backup plan. I'll be okay." She smiled, and Betty was certain that this remarkably beautiful young woman had once seen herself as the wife of the ailing Ivor Beame, who would then pass on to his reward, leaving his widow well fixed financially.

The maid appeared at the door. "I thought you'd gone. Mr. Beame doesn't like strangers hanging about."

"She's visiting with me, Lena," Miss Trouble said. "Mind your own business, not mine, or you won't have a job for long."

"I do have to return to the city," Betty said. She backed out of the room, leaving the two women glaring at each other.

It was a relief to get into the comfortable car, sit back, and let the driver take her to the hotel. Although it was not her assignment to assess Mr. Beame's nature, she concluded that he was very angry and very serious about righting the wrong that had been done to him. He was probably as ruthless as she had imagined him to be, and was only prevented from doing the righting himself by his age and infirmity. His mind was certainly sharp enough, and she knew she had to warn Ted about him. Then she wondered if she should express an opinion on what Ted was getting himself into. Surely it wasn't right to steal even from a ruthless businessman. She had assumed that Ted had higher standards.

She knew she had to call Ted as soon as she returned to the hotel. Maybe he knew what it was all about. It was certainly about more than sending him a warning about the stolen program.

Although it was only a bit after midday, the highway back into Manhattan was clogged with traffic. Betty wondered how commuters were willing to face such automotive chaos twice a day, and it wasn't even rush hour. Once they had to stop because of an accident. Fortunately, it was quickly cleared, but even in that short time an unmoving river of cars appeared behind the limo. This time they took a route that plunged them into a long tunnel, where bleak white-tile walls pressed in on them, the fluorescent lights gave their skin an unhealthy green color in spite of the tinted windows, and the smell of exhaust fumes seeped in.

Finally they were out of the tunnel and headed uptown, dodging traffic on Third Avenue. The car turned onto a side street and eventually halted in front of the Villa d'Este. Betty was starved, so she watched the car depart and then went to the coffee shop on the corner for a grilled cheese sandwich. Her wining and dining in New York hadn't been memorable so far, but she had hopes for her dinner with Lady Margaret and Gerald Toth.

Her first task was to telephone Ted to report on her meeting with Ivor Beame.

"He sounds as though he'll make trouble for you," Betty said. "He made some threats against both you and me. And there's this woman around him who seems to think he'll marry her and leave her his money after she's made arrangements to kill him off. A very unsavory group if you ask me. Are you sure you want to go ahead with this?"

"More than ever. Listen, Elizabeth, while I tell you a strange tale. As I mentioned, after I left you, I drove to Redding's Point. It was a real step back into my past, when I was a kid running around with the rest of the boys, sailing on the Sound, riding our bikes everywhere. Kids didn't have cars much in those days. I drove around a bit, having a look at the houses we used to rent. Nothing much changed, same old brown and gray cottages. Even my friend Stan Thurlow looked pretty unchanged himself. What I went there for was to retrieve something his two boys found at the same time they found the body of that drowned woman. A CD for a computer, it turned out to be. I suppose the very fact of finding such a thing on a beach is pretty odd, but here's the really odd part. I brought it home and looked at what was on it. It's part of Toth's ERP system, no question about it. So here's the puzzle: How did the dead woman get her hands on it? She must have been Toth's Xaviera. What was she doing in Connecticut? It's a pretty long way from New York. Who killed her? The boys didn't tell the police about the disc, and I'm not sure I want to turn it over to them until I have a chance to figure this out."

"But that's withholding evidence," Betty said. This whole business was turning into a real mess.

"I'm going to wait until I get the rest of the program from Toth. If the dead woman was his Xaviera, what does it all mean? She went to work for Ivor Beame, so did she help steal the software, only to give it to Toth? And why would she do that? Did Toth send her to Beame just to steal it? I can't see Beame allowing her to get near it. She was probably not a programmer, so she probably didn't have any standing at Beame's company. And then she was murdered. It's a real puzzle."

"Are you worried?"

"Yes," Ted said. "I have a feeling the woman was killed because of the disc, and now I have it. Well, I don't want to worry you, too. You enjoy yourself. But don't mention what I just told you to Toth until I have a chance to figure things out."

After she hung up, Betty thought she ought to have a little rest and then get ready to meet Lady Margaret for dinner.

She decided not to wear any of her fancier clothes for the evening's dinner, choosing instead a navy blazer and skirt and a nice flower-print blouse she'd bought for her brief stint as a substitute school secretary. She added one of the more distinguished brooches that Sid had given her. She thought again about the apparently enfeebled Ivor Beame, the lovely young woman she had spoken to, and what the maid had told her. Bunny Trouble sounded like a made-up name to her, although it might well have been made up by the maid. What was she? A trained nurse? She hadn't looked like a professional, of that sort at least, but of course Betty had only gotten brief glimpses of her. Gerald Toth might know about her, but no, she wouldn't ask, and in any case she wasn't sure she wanted Toth to know that she'd met with Ivor Beame. She hoped Lady Margaret wouldn't mention her phone call about her plans.

This was all becoming more of a challenge than she had anticipated. But she remembered what Sister Rita had said: Meet new challenges. She would.

She went down to the lobby a little before seven to wait for Lady Margaret. She tried to imagine what she'd look like. All she could picture were images of poor Princess Diana, then Fergie and the queen, all done up in regal robes and tiaras. That couldn't be right. English girls—even ladies—probably looked just like American girls.

Exactly at seven there was a flurry of activity, as the young man who seemed to have been assigned to give her messages and generally look after her was seen loping toward the hotel door, then greeting a nice-looking blond woman, medium height, rosy cheeks. She heard him say, "Milady, how good to see you at the Villa d'Este once again." They put their heads together and spoke a few words, then the young man guided her to where Betty was sitting. "Miss Trenka," he said, "here is Lady Margaret to see you." Betty was certainly scoring points with the hotel's staff because of all the significant people she seemed to know.

"How do you do?" Betty said. "How kind of you to take me out tonight."

"Hullo," Margaret said. "Lovely to meet you. Getting along in New York all right? Didn't have any problems with that man you were going to see, did you?"

"Not at all," Betty said, "but . . . if we're to meet Mr. Toth, I think it would be best if you didn't mention Ivor Beame. The two gentlemen seem to be business enemies. I don't really understand about all that, but . . ."

"Miss Trenka, I believe you understand quite well, but I will certainly not bring up the subject. Now, I thought we might try a nice new Italian place I know. It's quiet, and I know you need to get acquainted with Gerald a bit, so we won't be troubled by a crush of people, eavesdropping on our conversation."

"I'm sure anything you chose will be fine," Betty said.

"It's some distance away," Margaret said, "but I've persuaded Gerald to let me borrow his car. He will meet us at the restaurant." Betty was charmed by Lady Margaret's pronunciation of *restaurant*, making it sound rather French. Betty followed her out of the hotel and into an impressively luxurious town car. Betty found herself comparing it to Ivor Beame's and found it satisfactory. She was getting to be quite the automobile snob.

"Gerald doesn't own the car," Margaret said. "He hires it for the day or evening as needed. Since he doesn't live permanently in New York, I suppose he feels that owning and garaging an auto and maintaining a driver is a somewhat pointless expense." Margaret smiled charmingly. "Most of the society people I know who have their own cars in the city are seeking to raise themselves up in the eyes of the lower classes. It makes them appear wealthier than perhaps they really are, because everyone knows how expensive it is to keep a car in the city. Shall I have the driver take a route that will show you some of the city's sights?" She leaned forward and told him, "Go over to Fifth Avenue and down." Then she leaned back. "It's a fun street. You can catch a glimpse of the shops."

"I'd like that," Betty said, "although shops are not the heaven on earth for me that they are for some people."

Margaret was relieved. No lengthy shopping expeditions were called for. What, in fact, the driver did was to take them to Fifth Avenue at Fifty-Seventh Street, so that Margaret could point out the Plaza

Hotel, the edge of Central Park, Rockefeller Center on the right and St. Patrick's Cathedral on the left, then Saks Fifth Avenue. Farther down they passed the New York Public Library. When they reached the less interesting area below the library, Betty asked, "Do you know Mr. Toth well?"

"Well enough to call on him in times of trouble. We had . . . well, a romance of sorts a while back. Nothing serious, just a bit of fun going about together. I know he's very successful in his business, but it's a business I don't understand all that well. He seems to like to squire about attractive women—I don't refer to myself."

"But you are! You know, I've never met an actual lady before." Betty took a stab, since Lady Margaret wasn't wearing a wedding ring and she had confessed to a bit of a romance with Toth. "It must be that your father is an earl or higher, or however they grade that sort of thing."

"My late father was the Earl of Brayfield. My brother has the title now, and I came by the 'lady' honestly, but you shouldn't allow it to impress you unduly. Our home in England might impress you, though. Priam's Priory, it's called. It once housed a religious community before Henry the Eighth dissolved the monasteries and broke with the pope over his marital messes and search for power."

"Oh, yes," Betty said noncommittally. Years ago, when as a schoolgirl she had studied religious history, the stern nun who had taught the class had had noth-

ing good to say about Henry and his persecution of
the church. Instead she asked, "Then it's a Tudor
building?"

"Quite, and it's lovely. There are even some ruins
of the older original building, and bits of it are in-
corporated into the present one. We have two ghosts
and one of them is said to be a female religious who
inhabited the place back in Henry's day. There are
still some old records in our library about her, and
modern-day visitors who come upon our ghost are
required to record their sightings, so we have a history of her appearances going back several cen-
turies."

"Have you seen the ghost?" Betty wasn't sure she
believed in ghosts, but if Lady Margaret said they ex-
isted, she wasn't going to argue.

Margaret shrugged. "I think so, although my
mother insisted that the stresses of puberty made me
imagine it. I know what I saw, and once not long ago
both our ghosts were helpful in solving a murder that
took place at the priory. Do you find this nonsense?"

"Not at all," Betty said. "It's fascinating. I'd love
to see Priam's Priory someday." She would spend
whatever she earned from Ted's assignment on a trip
to England in the spring, she decided suddenly. It all
sounded so intriguing.

"Perhaps you shall," Margaret said. "My poor
brother spends a good deal of time trying to find the
money to keep the place in good order, and he may
decide he'll have to open the house to visitors, to

earn a few pounds or Euros or whatever we'll be using. But you, of course, wouldn't be asked to pay admission. I'd see that you were honored as my guest. Ah, here we are."

Betty was not impressed by the neighborhood. It seemed to be a dark street lined with warehouses. There were several stretch limos lining the curb, and some nicely dressed people were entering one of the warehouses through a heavy door with brass fittings. There was a brass plaque beside the entrance, but it was too small for Betty to read, even with her glasses.

"It's a fairly new place, but it quickly became very popular. Restaurants open and close in New York like blinking eyelids. I'm glad this place has managed to stay in business for a few months. I was introduced to it by a lovely young man and a good friend, Prince Paul Castrocani. Ah, you know his mother, of course. Carolyn Sue Hoopes."

"I don't really know Mrs. Hoopes," Betty said. "My connection with her was made through my . . . employer, Ted Kelso, who seems to know Mr. Hoopes. He did mention that Carolyn Sue had been a princess."

"Indeed she was. I must have you meet Prince Paul. I say, I've made arrangements for us to attend a charity function tomorrow evening. I'll see that Paul is there to meet you. Are you free to join us? It might be a bit formal."

"That wouldn't be a problem," Betty said. "I came prepared for anything New York has to offer."

"I hope not everything," Margaret said. "Gerald and I were threatened by a crazed woman with a gun Saturday evening. I hope her passions have cooled by now and she won't know where to find us tonight. Fortunately, he had a bodyguard with him. I hope the bodyguard's around tonight as well. Come along, I don't want to keep Gerald waiting, and the restaurant is very particular about people arriving on time for their reservations."

The interior was quite unlike its bleak exterior. There were a sea of tables with white tablecloths, many handsomely dressed and coiffed diners, a horde of black-jacketed waiters, huge arrangements of flowers, and tiny candles on each table. The most delicious aromas greeted them.

The walls consisted of long, intricate murals depicting what seemed to be barely clothed Roman gods and goddesses frolicking in a romantic-looking forest glade.

"We have a reservation for three," Margaret told the maître d'. "Lady Margaret Priam. I wonder if our third has arrived."

The maître d' was as glossy and black-and-white and smug as a pampered Boston terrier. "How nice to see you again, Lady Margaret. Is it Prince Paul who's joining you?"

"No, Gerald Toth. Ah, I see him at the bar. There at the end."

"I'll have a waiter bring him to your table. This way, Lady Margaret." Betty was apparently invisible to him. They were seated and the maître d' fawned over Margaret for a few moments longer, then Gerald Toth approached. He was indeed as startlingly handsome as advertised, and when he turned his amazingly blue eyes on Betty, she felt a weakness in her knees that she hadn't experienced since she was a teenager gazing at Cary Grant on the movie screen.

"Margaret darling"—he kissed her cheek briefly—"and you must be Elizabeth Trenka." He shook her hand and favored her with a long look. What was it Ted had said? Women melt when he smiles. She knew now what he'd meant. "What a treat to see you both."

"Treat" was stretching it a bit, Betty thought, although Gerald Toth and Margaret did make a handsome couple.

He sat and they read the menu. Betty was dazzled by the array of dishes offered but noticed uneasily that everything was in Italian. Well, she did recognize the names of some of the pastas, but the dishes featuring *maiale, abbacchio, fegato, gamberetti, melanzane, anitra*, and *manzo* stopped her. Ah, *pollo*. She recognized chicken. Suddenly, she felt very stupid and wondered how she would manage when she took her long-dreamed-of trip to Europe and found herself facing starvation because she didn't know what to order.

Margaret said kindly, "It's a rather daunting menu, isn't it? Can I suggest some choices, Miss Trenka?"

Betty smiled her appreciation of the offer. "I'm afraid East Moulton doesn't offer most of these things." Indeed, spaghetti with a thick red sauce and hefty meatballs was about the best the town diner could offer in the way of Italian fare.

At Gerald's insistence they ordered far too much food, all of it very expensive.

"Miss Trenka would, I think, enjoy the lumachelle al tartufo," Margaret said, "and then the saltimbocca alla Romana." She explained. "Lumachelle are pasta shaped liked snails, a bit like elbow macaroni with a curve on one end so that they look like snails. They're served with a black truffle sauce that is divine. Saltimbocca is veal scallops with proscuitto and sage—a Roman specialty that Prince Paul loves. The truffle sauce comes from Umbria, where there are truffles all over the place."

Gerald chose risotto with lobster and shrimp and roasted baby lamb, another Roman specialty, Margaret told her, while Margaret herself ordered quadrucci in brodo and quail with grapes.

"Wait until you see the quadrucci," she said. "It's a beautiful dish."

Gerald perused the wine list, debated the virtues of several vintages with Margaret, and then chose the one he preferred. The waiter brought bottled water, thick slices of bread, and a dish of olive oil instead of butter. He also placed a plate of raw vegetables on the table—scallions, asparagus, baby artichokes, zucchini, fennel, carrots, and endive—along with a bowl of dipping sauce, which turned out to be flavored with garlic and anchovies.

"I took the liberty of ordering the bagna cauda while I was waiting," Gerald said to Margaret. "My experience with models has taught me that ladies find vegetables more alluring than cheese and salami."

They sampled the vegetables, and soon enough the first course arrived. The lumachelle in truffle sauce was heavenly, and Margaret's soup contained thin squares of pasta with pale green shadows of leaves that almost looked like embroidery.

"It's parsley leaves pressed into the pasta dough," Margaret said. "Aren't they lovely?"

The food kept coming, and Gerald fussed about Margaret: did she like the quail, did she want vegetables or a salad, was the wine acceptable?

"Gerald, don't worry about me, worry about our visitor."

"Miss Trenka—" Gerald Toth turned his attention from Margaret to Betty at last.

"Please, both of you, call me Elizabeth."

"Well, Elizabeth, I think we can save our business discussion until tomorrow and just concentrate on having a pleasant meal tonight." But he didn't. "Have you worked in the information technology field for long?"

Betty took a deep mental breath and said, "For a time, but I'm an administrative person rather than a technical one."

"But surely if you work with Ted Kelso you've picked up a great deal."

But before Betty could think of how to answer him, Gerald was on his feet. "That damned woman," he said. "She's stalking me. Let me just see to this." He moved quickly away from the table and went to the maître d's station, where a slim, blond woman was arguing with the manager of the restaurant. Gerald Toth took her arm firmly and propelled her toward the door. She seemed to resist at first but finally allowed herself to be escorted off the premises. Gerald followed her out the door.

"Goodness, that one again," Margaret said. "I hope she's left her gun at home."

"Trouble," Betty murmured. "I hope so as well." She had felt slightly intimidated by the restaurant, the haughty maître d', the officious waiters, and the scampering busboys who refilled water glasses that didn't need refilling and removed cutlery and plates that were barely used, replacing them with fresh ones. Now she was relaxed, and even the appearance of Miss Trouble, with or without a gun, seemed merely routine. Perhaps Betty was meeting Sister Rita's expectation that she would face challenges and overcome them, although surely Sister Rita hadn't had this high-class dining place in mind.

"I'm afraid she is rather a spot of trouble," Margaret said. "She's the one who tried to shoot us on Saturday evening. But not to worry. Gerald will handle her."

"No, I meant that's her name, Trouble, or something like it. And I've seen her before. I even had a chat with her. She was at Ivor Beame's house on Long Island today. Apparently her duties as a caregiver cease at sundown. Who is she really? Do you know?"

"A model named Brunetta," Margaret said. "They're a very unpredictable class of people."

CHAPTER 12

GERALD TOTH returned, having disposed of the young woman without too much fuss. Betty wanted to ask more about her, about the gun and the attempted shooting Lady Margaret had mentioned in connection with her, but she thought it wouldn't be appropriate. Betty also decided not to discuss seeing the woman at Ivor Beame's home, at least not just yet.

"Sorry about the distraction," Gerald said. "Just someone with a grudge. I never knew Brunetta had the wit to follow someone on her own. Very clever of her. I also wonder how she knew we were here." Then he seemed to feel it was time to drop the subject. "I hope everyone has room for dessert. Tiramisù. I understand it's one of their specialties. This place was just about the first to serve it before it became the mainstay of every Italian restaurant in town, not to mention selected Greek diners." Betty had seen the dessert mentioned in a restaurant review, but it hadn't appeared at East Moulton's few dining spots, none of which were Italian in any case, so she was looking forward to trying it. "More wine, Miss Trenka? Or we could order you a glass of champagne."

"I don't think I need more to drink, Mr. Toth. The wine you selected for dinner was excellent, however." She hoped he and Margaret would discuss Miss Trouble a bit, but he turned the conversation to business matters.

"I suppose you know Ted Kelso well."

"Of course. Ted is both a colleague and a neighbor," Betty said carefully. "As I'm sure you know, he is slightly disabled, so it is convenient for me to be close at hand since he prefers not to leave his home on a regular basis."

"He was quite the hotshot in the programming world back when he was healthy," Gerald said. "I suppose you don't lose the gift just because you can't run a five-K race any longer. I wouldn't be hiring him for this project if I thought he couldn't do it."

He wasn't doing a very good job of not talking business.

Betty tried to see behind his handsome face and gracious manners, but there was no way she could determine anything about him. Perhaps their discussion tomorrow would be more revealing, but she suspected he was good at not allowing people behind that facade. Now he was being attentive to Margaret again.

Margaret said unexpectedly, "Did you know that

Elizabeth saw your dangerous lady friend earlier to-day?"

Gerald's head whipped around to look at Betty. "You know Brunetta?"

"No, no, of course not," Betty said. "I just happened to be in the same place she was." She was uncomfortable about admitting that she'd seen his archrival, Ivor Beame, but she was grateful to Margaret for giving her the opening. The longer she kept silent about it, the more uncomfortable she'd be if and when Gerald learned about the meeting.

"The oddest thing happened when I arrived in New York yesterday, Mr. Toth. A Mr. Ivor Beame, whose name I had heard perhaps once before, somehow knew that I was here and why. So he invited me to meet with him at his home on Long Island today. I really didn't know who he was, but I went, and we talked about . . . things." She took a deep breath. "We actually discussed his belief that the program you want Ted to work on was stolen. I wasn't convinced, so I let it pass. When I was leaving, I happened to notice a young woman that I first took to be his granddaughter, but the maid called her Mr. Beame's caregiver—he's quite elderly and not strong, a heart condition was mentioned—and then referred to her as Bunny Trouble. I had a brief chat with her." But she wasn't going to tell him what the subject was.

Gerald Toth started to laugh, but it wasn't a joyful sound at all. "So Brunetta has her eye on the Beame millions, which are in the hands of an ailing old man." His mirth vanished quickly. "Brunetta's last name is Trumbull, and her given name actually is Bunny. She uses Brunetta as a professional name for her modeling career. But I had no idea that she'd hooked up with Beame." He frowned. "If that's the case, it might explain her actions the other night. I never believed that she was so attached to me, Margaret, that she couldn't bear to see me with another woman and would resort to firearms to halt it. But now it seems entirely possible that she was looking out for Beame's interests."

Then he used his cell phone to place a call. Betty heard him say, "Sonny, I think you ought to come over here. I'm at Risotto on West Sixteenth Street. It's right off Fifth. Wait in the car for me. He's parked right outside. That woman is on the loose again." He nodded to Margaret as he stowed his cell phone. "Protection is on the way. They won't allow her back into the restaurant tonight, and Sonny will be here shortly. I am truly sorry that my personal business is interfering with this pleasant evening. I apologize to you, Elizabeth."

Betty only half heard him. She was beginning to feel sleepy from the wine she'd drunk and the food she'd consumed. Wining and dining could be very tiring. "It's no problem," she said. "I didn't expect this evening to be all business, but it certainly has been interesting. Anyhow, I'm not really prepared for a serious discussion. We'll do that tomorrow."

"An early start," Gerald said. "I'll have the car pick you up at ten. Is that too early?"

She shook her head. "I'm always up with the dawn. I have a cat that . . ." She decided that nobody cared about Tina's role in her life. "I was expected at my office by eight, so I don't sleep in, even now that I'm retired. There are always so many things to do." That wasn't true, but Margaret and Gerald didn't know that.

"And don't forget that you and Paul and I are going to mix with the upper classes of society in the evening," Margaret said. "I hope you won't be too tired after working all day with Gerald."

"It's not a lot of work," he said. "Mostly talk. I'd like to get an idea of what Miss Trenka is like."

How odd, Betty thought, that he wants to do about me what I'm supposed to do about him. Maybe he thinks I'll let slip information that Ted has shared with me. Maybe . . . She felt herself on the edge of dozing and shook her head to keep herself alert.

Margaret noticed and said, "Maybe we should get Elizabeth home to bed. She's had a full day."

"Not until Sonny gets here," Gerald said, and he said it firmly. "And our dessert."

The tiramisù was delicious. Betty detected the flavor of some sort of brandy and the creamy texture of custard between layers of ladyfingers. But she was glad to know that they would soon be leaving.

"Ah, there's Sonny just arriving." Gerald summoned the waiter and paid the bill with a silver credit card. The waiter's eyes widened when he saw the size of his tip. They met Sonny at the door. Betty didn't know exactly what a bodyguard was supposed to look like, but she thought Sonny filled the bill. He reminded her of a prizefighter whose doctor hadn't quite succeeded in reconstructing his broken nose.

"Nobody hanging around outside," he said. "Your driver saw her walking over toward Fifth some time ago. Probably went to pick up a cab to take her to wherever those skinny broads like to spend their time being entertained by the kind of scum who hang with models." He didn't seem aware of the insult to Gerald Toth, who liked to hang with models, and Gerald simply ignored the remark.

The ride back to the hotel was short. Betty wasn't interested in looking at any more sights, and Margaret and Gerald conversed in low tones apparently about mutual friends in New York. Betty heard him trying to persuade Margaret not to end the evening but to go elsewhere with him.

Betty said suddenly, "Mr. Beame seemed to know all about me, where I used to work, where I lived, and so forth. It made me uneasy to think someone had bothered to find it all out."

"Ivor Beame is a very careful man. He knows that Ted is going to be working with me, so he certainly would try to learn as much about Ted's associates as possible. Miss Trenka, I should warn you. Ivor is not my friend."

"That was clear," Betty said. "Ah, here's the hotel. I do want to thank you both for a lovely evening. No, please don't get out. I can manage."

"Until tomorrow," Gerald said.

"I'll ring you in the afternoon about the party," Margaret said.

They watched Betty nod to the doorman, who pushed the revolving door for her, and she disappeared into the Villa d'Este.

"She's a terribly nice woman," Margaret said. "I do hope no one will try to harm her. It wouldn't be fair to bring her to New York and then have your business affairs do her some damage."

"I didn't bring her to New York," Gerald said. "It was Ted Kelso's idea entirely. I haven't quite figured out what he's up to, but he's no fool. Nor, I imagine, is Miss Trenka. Since you won't go out somewhere with me, we'll just drop you home. I don't think that bloodthirsty bitch has any interest in doing you in, but she might be waiting outside my door. She's scary, but, you know, it makes her all the more appealing to me. Margaret, help me out here. Why did I fall for the likes of Brunetta? Why did I fall for Xaviera?"

"Well, Brunetta is sensationally beautiful. I wouldn't know about your Xaviera."

"She was great-looking and smart, which Brunetta

isn't. I suppose looks have something to do with it, but maybe there's some sense of . . . what would you call it? Not danger, but the danger of being abandoned by someone I've put a lot of emotion into. I don't know why Bru has gotten herself involved with Beame. I have lots more money than he does."

"Money isn't everything, Gerald. I'm sure you're much better-looking than he is."

"Thank you for your support, my dear. You sound uncertain on the question of looks. But you're correct, if I do say so myself. Beame is seventy at least, and was never a poster boy, even in his younger days."

"But as you hinted, he's much closer to not needing his money than you are. Brunetta isn't dumb."

"Yes," he said, "yes, she is, but even she can grasp that a man with a heart condition is not likely to live forever. I'll arrange for you to meet her one day, and you'll see."

"If she doesn't shoot you first."

"She wouldn't, not unless Beame is paying her a lot of money to do so."

Margaret was dropped at her towering apartment building on the Upper East Side, and Gerald, guarded by an apparently dozing Sonny sitting up in front with the driver, watched her enter the lobby of her building safely.

His cell phone buzzed politely. He hated to receive calls he wasn't expecting, although he was responsible for a lot of business interests. His people in California worked late and weren't concerned about the three-hour time difference, but it was after business hours even now in California. So what if the boss decided to go to sleep early, we need to know *now*. He answered, expecting to hear his assistant, Janis, complaining about someone who hadn't done something he or she was supposed to do. He half hoped it would be Brunetta, but he'd been rather harsh to her outside the restaurant and he didn't think she would have gotten over her kicked-puppy mood so quickly. Most likely she was vamping her way through a crowd of transvestites and flavor-of-the-second boy movie-starlets at some noisy downtown club. She'd think she was showing him that she didn't need his attentions.

"Hello," he said.

"Gerry, glad I got through to you. You were supposed to call me." For a minute Gerald couldn't identify the male voice. Then he realized it was Elliott, the weak link in his slightly illegal business plan. "I, like, kind of need the money you owe me. Any way I can see you tonight? Now?"

"Elliott, no, for a lot of reasons. I'm in a car in the middle of traffic. That's one reason. Two, the kind of money we were talking about isn't something I carry around in the car in a briefcase. I've been making some arrangements and I was supposed to call you when they were set up. And I will."

"Better be soon, Gerry. I need it right away."

"I'll do the best I can, Elliott. But remember, I'm

paying you both for what you brought me and for your silence. Don't go talking about our deal to anybody. Beame's out to get us both and I have protection. You don't."

"Don't worry about me, kiddo. I can take care of myself."

"How did you get this number anyhow? It's strictly for private calls."

"Maybe I got it from one of your private callers," Elliott said.

Not likely, Gerald thought, but they were close to his building, and he wanted to get Elliott off the line before he went inside. "Look, Elliott, I can't talk now. I have . . . someone with me."

"I hope it's not that twisted skinny dame you like so much."

"What do you know about that? It's a personal matter."

"I know her is all. I was kinda thinking that if you paid me what you owe, I might have a go at her myself. Money matters to her."

Gerald tried to imagine the exquisite Brunetta being so enamored of cash that she would consider consorting with the geeky Elliott, who had no outward appeal at all and hadn't much conversation beyond the virtues and drawbacks of certain computer programming languages. Languages that Brunetta didn't speak. Still, Xaviera had found him worth talking to. Women were impossible to understand.

"I don't think Bru's quite your type," Gerald said,

"although she is, as you say, a bit twisted." The car had pulled up to the curb in front of his building, and Sonny had slid out and was doing a quick inspection tour of the street and the nooks and crannies of nearby buildings. He rousted a homeless man who had moved his sheet of cardboard into a corner near the steps of a neighboring building, but otherwise the street seemed empty and quiet.

"Gotta go, Elliott. I'll call you as soon as there's something. Should be this week."

"Make that *will be* this week, and I'm cool." Elliott hung up, and Gerald pushed a button on his cell phone and put it away. He might even kill Brunetta for handing out his cell phone number to a lowlife like Elliott, who obviously had a crush on her. Then he remembered sadly that when Elliott had come over to the company with the Ivor Enterprises program, he had also been very tight with Xaviera before she disappeared. They were always giggling and joking, like old friends. He still resented that, and he could still see the two of them kidding around while he stood in the doorway to his office watching. Xaviera knew he was there, but she kept tossing her hair and flashing a smile at Elliott, who ate up the attention and blushed when she put her hand on his arm. The hand with that magnificent ring Gerald had given her.

Gerald Toth blinked back tears. He'd really cared about the woman, even if she had been in league with Elliott.

It had made him sick to see them together, and it

was after an argument about Elliott that Xaviera had packed up and gone away. Well, she was gone for good now, and he had more important matters to handle.

He had to get the CDs with the ERP program up to Ted in Connecticut as soon as possible, and Ted had to check the program out, maybe make some changes so that it wouldn't be identical to the one Elliott had removed from Beame's company and handed over to Xaviera Corporation. For a steep price. He'd worry about it tomorrow, after he'd talked to Miss Trenka. He would, he decided, have her hand-carry the CDs to Ted rather than entrust them to one of the overnight carriers.

Gerald got the all-clear from Sonny, and the two men walked into the building. The limo driver eased away, back to his garage in Queens.

Betty was already wrapping herself in her pink robe, and Margaret was checking her phone messages. There was one from De Vere, which pleased her. He had had some free time that evening and had hoped for some time with her. Too late to call him back tonight. She also had a message from Paul Castrocani, saying he was doing nothing the next evening except accompanying her and her visitor from Connecticut to the charity reception "as long as I'm not expected to pay for a ticket. Funds are short, and my dear mother has vanished into the desert to commune with her advisers on the matter of exfoliation. She did not remember to have my allowance check sent to me."

Dear Paul had lived a life of luxury before his indulgent mother had married Ben Hoopes, who did not like to see his wife's wealth squandered on an unemployable bit of Eurotrash like his stepson Paul. In recent years Paul had had to make do with a—to him—modest allowance and the occasional jobs found for him by his stepfather. His father, Prince Aldo, was as impoverished as only a titled Italian can be, so he had nothing to give his son. Paul's employment adventures never lasted long, because he had never learned a trade or a profession except to be, for society hostesses, a welcome single young man in his late twenties with good manners and good looks. The ideal table filler, in fact. Margaret was very fond of Paul in an entirely sisterly way. Indeed, she felt more like a sister to Paul than she did to her own brother, who was back home in England trying to keep Priam's Priory afloat and seeking a suitable wife to become the next Countess of Brayfield.

No more messages. She thought about Gerald and was glad to know that the days when she had thrilled to the touch of his hand were safely in the past. She did like him, though, and she thought his infatuation with Brunetta—Miss Trouble, as Elizabeth had called her—was ill-advised. Surely a man of Gerald's position needed someone with more substance. Maybe she should try to find him a suitable woman. With that goal swirling in her head, she retired, along with the rest of the evening's cast.

CHAPTER 13

THE NEXT morning Betty decided she shouldn't waste her time in New York hanging around her hotel. As soon as she finished her meeting with Gerald Toth, she intended to go out and see some sights.

She indulged herself with a room-service breakfast and then she knew she should call Ted to tell him about her dinner with Gerald Toth.

First she phoned the nursing home in Connecticut and reassured Ellie that she was fine. Ellie promised to tell Sid. "He's doing okay today," she said. "One of his good days."

Ted listened to her tale of the dinner with Gerald and Margaret at which the same young woman she had seen at Ivor Beame's house had appeared and seemed agitated, even threatening. Gerald and Margaret had talked of seeing her with a gun in her hands. "They called her Brunetta Trumbull." In the background Betty could hear Ted tapping out something on his keyboard.

"What do you think of them all?" Ted asked.

"Lady Margaret is charming," Betty said. "A real lady, if you know what I mean. Mr. Beame is accustomed to having his way. He appears to be aged and weak, but I doubt that applies to his mind. I believe he's capable of anything. I sensed that he is deeply angry about something."

"Me, Gerald Toth. As well he might be," Ted said. "And Toth?"

"I hesitate to offer an opinion. Yet. His car is picking me up in half an hour for our meeting. I'll report promptly, I promise. First impression? He enjoys his money, likes to throw his weight around. He has a bodyguard, by the way, so apparently he feels himself to be in danger."

"As well he might be," Ted repeated. "I'll wait to hear from you, although I did hear from Toth myself early this morning. He's pressing me to accept his offer, wondered why I'd sent an unknowledgeable person like you to speak with him."

"I told him I didn't know about technical things," Betty said, slightly offended by Gerald Toth's assessment of her. "I said I was on the administrative side." She'd show him.

"Just be careful, Elizabeth. It appears that things are heating up. Keep your ears open for the name Elliott Wolfson. He's the guy who stole the software and brought it to Xaviera. And, it says here, your Miss Trumbull is in actuality a very highly paid and very well-known model. She even has her own Web site. If you paid more attention to the big fashion magazines, you would probably have recognized her from their covers. Wonder what she is to Gerald Toth?"

"I had the impression that he is or was quite infatuated with her. He didn't offer an opinion as to why she happened to be hanging about Mr. Beame's house. The maid called her a caregiver, as though he was housebound and in need of constant care. But that couldn't be entirely true, as he himself came to my hotel to leave me a message the day I arrived, one of the young men who work here said so. What I think is that Miss Trumbull has decided that she should be the next Mrs. Beame, at which time she will cease to care for him and pray for another heart attack. Perhaps Mr. Beame will go ahead with a marriage. It would be a way of getting even with Mr. Toth for the theft of his software. And I should imagine that Mr. Toth would not enjoy seeing his favored beauty scooped up by his rival. They are none of them very nice people, Ted."

"Just be careful and try to have a good time."

"I will. Lady Margaret is taking me to a charity reception tonight."

"Don't get carried away by the social ramble, Elizabeth. It's not healthy."

She finished the call and rushed to dress in one of her old business suits with sensible shoes. And one of the lovely rings Sid had given her, so she'd feel he was with her during the meeting.

The front desk rang her before she had a chance to

go down to the lobby. "Your car is here, Miss Trenka."

"I'm on my way," Betty said. She took one more look in the mirror and thought she looked professional and as knowledgeable as she was likely to get.

It was a very short ride from the Villa d'Este to the brownstone building on a cross street. She mounted the steps and looked at the buzzers near the door. Apparently there were three apartments, but none of the names listed was Toth. As she was deciding which button to push, Sonny, the bodyguard, opened the door.

"Good morning, Miss Trenka," he said. "It's one flight up, or there's an elevator, which you couldn't pay me to take."

"I'll walk up," Betty said. The carpeted stairs and the highly polished banister were easy enough, and Sonny followed behind her. At the head of the stairs, he pointed to a door that was slightly ajar, and they went inside. Betty expected the ultimate in luxury, if Gerald Toth was as wealthy as everyone said, but it was a simply furnished place. Sonny indicated that she should go into a room to the left, and she found herself in a comfortable study with a huge TV set, a music system, and a desk with two computers.

"He's coming right now," Sonny said, and withdrew, closing the door behind him. Betty looked around. It was an impersonal room, and except for a pile of papers on the desk and a briefcase on the floor beside it, there was little to say that Gerald Toth worked here. Then she noticed on the desk the silver picture frame facing the big leather chair. It was a portrait of Brunetta, looking her most glamorous. Betty glanced at the desk and was startled to see another picture of Brunetta on top of the pile of papers. This picture, however, had a big red X across her face. Love/hate? Or something else?

She looked away guiltily as Toth entered the study. "Good morning, good morning. I'm afraid I don't have too much time to spare after all. Please have a seat and tell me what you want of me."

Betty had prepared her "interview" questions in advance and kept them in her head, but she made a show of taking a sheet of paper from her handbag— blank, of course—and looking it over. "Ted has asked me to query you about the provenance of the software you want him to test. How long has Xaviera Corporation been developing it? When is the expected release date, that is, after he has finished testing it, and so forth? Do you have orders for it, and if so, what size are the companies? He said he wasn't interested in the company names, which might well be privileged information. That's it for starters." She folded her paper and put it away.

Toth smiled. "Not taking notes, Miss Trenka?"

"My memory is excellent," she said, and waited for his answers. Although he was facing her across the desk, she felt her suspicions rising. He wouldn't meet her eyes.

"How long has it been in development? Years. It's

a very complex program. And years longer since I got the idea for it. It took a while to figure out exactly what the market was and how to handle the components, then find the right person to start working on it."

"And who would that be? I'm afraid I don't know anybody in the business, but Ted might. He said knowing who worked on the code would give him an idea of how it was handled and where any bugs might be."

"I shouldn't think Ted would know of him," Toth said offhandedly. "He's extremely bright, but a typically oddball computer type, not a public figure. Programmers are often very reticent about their work."

His phone buzzed. "Excuse the interruption." He picked up the phone and swung around in his chair so that its high back muffled the conversation, but Betty managed to overhear it. "I already told you when. Look, I'm in a meeting now." Toth sounded annoyed. "Listen, Elliott, I don't like threats. Not from you, not from anybody."

Betty noted the name *Elliott* coupled with the word *threats*. It sounded like blackmail to her, but she was examining the handsome silver letter opener that lay on the desk when Toth finished his call and turned the chair around.

"A disgruntled former employee complaining about vacation back pay," Toth said smoothly. "I wish these people would call our human resources department out in California instead of bothering me. He probably wanted to save a few pennies by making a local call." He still wouldn't meet her eyes. "Now what else was it you wanted to know? Orders? Well, word has gotten out about our ERP software. That's an Enterprise Resource Planning system. It helps companies connect all their various systems under one program. It's especially useful when companies merge and there are a lot of resources to combine so they'll all work together, and it's a big help in streamlining e-commerce—the Internet and other electronic business dealings. Xaviera has a good reputation for offering the best product, so yes, we have quite a few orders, and we'll make a lot of money. The interested companies are of all sizes and types, Fortune 500, some promising startups, and then there are some big ones that have gotten bigger through mergers. Really, Miss Trenka, this seems to be a fairly pointless exercise. You clearly have no understanding of the technology involved or the implications of our ERP in the commercial world. I don't know why Ted bothered to send you to New York."

Betty bristled. She had never taken kindly to gratuitous insults. She sat up straight in her chair and looked him in the eye. This time he did not look away. "Mr. Toth, it may well be that I have purposes that you are not aware of. Do not underestimate me. I know quite enough to understand what you are telling me, even if I couldn't write a program to save my soul. I understand that you couldn't do it either."

"And just what might your purposes be, Miss Trenka?"

"That is confidential, but I believe I have achieved my goals." She would tell Ted that Toth was a bully and a fluent liar. She thought that Molly Perkins at the pharmacy could come up with a better story than that back-pay one. She wasn't sure what her next question should be, so she said, "Why would anyone want to deface a lovely picture of Miss Trumbull?"

Toth looked at her hard and his hand reached out for the photograph. He crumpled it and tossed it away. "Someone's idea of a joke," he said. "A jealous suitor probably. I've been seeing Brunetta on and off for the past few weeks, and she's very attractive to men. It might even be Beame."

"He doesn't seem the sort to send that type of message. I imagine he's more likely to simply state his mind or take steps to eliminate you as a rival. I believe he has a certain deep attachment to Brunetta as well."

Toth narrowed his eyes at her, then shifted some papers on his desk. "Beame and I have been business rivals for years, but I have scarcely met him face-to-face." He changed the subject abruptly. "I have something I want you to take back to Connecticut for Ted. It's very valuable, indeed, so you must guard it well." He removed a flat plastic box from a drawer. It was the sort of box that held music CDs. He snapped it open and showed her the silver discs with golden highlights. "These CD-ROMs are worth a few million to others." He looked at each disc carefully, then drew in his breath sharply. He took the discs out of the box and examined them, paying no attention to Betty. She saw three discs, each marked with a large X and some other printing.

Betty hesitated. "I wonder if you shouldn't entrust those things to . . . to someone like Sonny. He could take the train to New Haven, and I'm sure Ted would meet him there and take possession. I don't know that I am capable of the heroics that might be necessary to keep that box out of others' hands. And what if something happened? Say I lost it."

"It isn't the only copy in existence, Miss Trenka. I had another copy burned and it's safe in California. This is just the only copy I'm allowing out of my hands. You can put the box in a locked safe-deposit box at the hotel until you leave." He stood. "I don't imagine we'll have occasion to meet again during your visit."

It sounded as though he was ending their meeting. And she still had only partly accomplished what she'd been sent to New York to do: to determine whether Gerald Toth was trustworthy. He was certainly a criminal for accepting the stolen software. Well, she supposed that said a good deal about his ethical standards. He was the object of a certain amount of animosity—Brunetta and Ivor Beame, to name just two, and there were surely others.

"I'm going to be here for several more days," she

said. "But if you're determined to give the CDs to me now . . ." She shrugged. "I guess I have no choice."

"There is a message I'd like you to give Ted as soon as you hand these over to him. Tell him three of four is missing. I think I know where it is, and I'll see that he gets it promptly. I'm glad to see you're not writing that down."

"Three of four is missing, and he'll get it promptly. How's that?"

She glanced up to see a smile of satisfaction on his face, but his eyes were focused on a spot above her head.

"That's the spirit," he said. "Let me call the car for you, and you can get on with being a tourist."

Sonny was at the door to see her out, and he looked up and down the street before he nodded for her to descend the steps and enter the car, the door of which was being held open by the driver. Betty decided she could easily get accustomed to being driven everywhere in a luxury town car, which was not necessarily a good thing. It made her faithful Buick seem shabby. She was determined to try the New York subways when she ventured out to sightsee.

Before the car pulled away, she watched as Sonny sprinted down the street ahead of them and accosted a young man in jeans and a denim jacket, rumpled hair, and thick glasses. The young man didn't appear to be doing anything except leaning on a wrought-iron gate leading to the ground floor of another brownstone. Sonny grasped his shoulder and appeared to be speaking to him rapidly. Then the town car passed them and turned onto the avenue, and Betty could see who the boy was. It was the young man who seemed to be following her.

Betty glanced through a New York guidebook that she'd found at a newsstand next to the coffee shop and selected Times Square as her first sight. The subway map didn't show any lines near the Villa d'Este—she'd have to go over to Lexington Avenue to find a subway—but the map showed a bus line going down Second Avenue past Forty-second Street, where she could change to a crosstown bus that would take her to Times Square. She made certain that she had exact change for the bus fare and ventured out of her room. She surrendered the precious CD case to her friend behind the registration desk with the instructions that it be locked up in the hotel's safe-deposit box.

"There's a safe in your room, Miss Trenka," her young man said.

"I'd prefer not to leave it in my room. It's not my property, and I'd rather the hotel was in charge of it."

It was a warm day for early fall, and although it was a workday, there were quite a few pedestrians on Second Avenue. She realized that it was the lunch hour, but after last evening's Italian feast and her hearty breakfast, she chose to skip the meal for the present. Perhaps she would enjoy the English tea the hotel advertised later in the afternoon. She spotted the bus shelter a block down the avenue but didn't notice the young man in jeans and a denim jacket who strolled behind her. Two buses with blue New York City Transit logos were stopped at the traffic light before the bus shelter, and when she got on the first one, the young man entered the second one. Betty clutched her transfer and watched the numbered street signs pass by. At Forty-second Street she got out and crossed over to the shelter where she could catch the crosstown bus.

"Will you announce Times Square?" she asked the driver.

"You can't miss it, lady. Yeah, I'll tell you."

They passed the Chrysler Building and Grand Central Station. She glimpsed a sign saying Madison Avenue, then saw the New York Public Library on Fifth Avenue. Behind it was Bryant Park, which stretched to Sixth Avenue, labeled in her guidebook as Avenue of the Americas. After the bus crossed Sixth, the driver said, "Times Square next stop."

He was right. You couldn't mistake it for anything else. It was just as she'd remembered it from her long-ago visits to New York and the television pictures on New Year's Eve. There was a Warner Brothers store, a Disney store, and a huge yellow sign for *The Lion King*. There were new skyscrapers under construction, a million billboards and lighted signs, plenty of people and congested traffic. She walked up Broadway, glancing down the side streets at the theater marquees. When she saw the sign for *The Serpent's Tooth . . . King Lear: The Musical,* she turned down the street. There didn't appear to be a lot of activity at the box office. Perhaps the idea of *Lear* with lyrics hadn't struck a chord with New York theatergoers. Still, she bought a ticket for Thursday evening and wondered if she ought to invite Lady Margaret. She thought not. The poor woman probably had much better things to do than follow her around. She felt quite capable of getting herself to the theater and back even without Gerald Toth's car.

Back on Broadway, she looked at the hordes of people rushing this way and that. There was a man orating on a traffic island while a small crowd listened to his shrill, electronically enhanced voice. She noticed quite a few young people on the streets, boys with baggy jeans, girls in trendy-looking outfits. She wondered if the latter were the runaways she'd heard so much about. The boys looked tough and confident, as though Times Square was their home turf. There were a few "adult" movie theaters to be seen and several women in suggestive clothes who could be prostitutes, but she didn't see that they were attracting much attention. Well, she'd read that Times Square had been "cleaned up," whatever that meant. At street level, cleanliness didn't seem immediately apparent, but perhaps the newspaper hadn't been talking about actual street cleaning and trash removal.

She saw a number of entrances to the subway but

decided against that adventure for the moment. She wanted to study a subway map and understand exactly where she was going before she attempted it. The marquees of the many movie theaters heralded the latest films, few of which had reached the multiplex at the mall near East Moulton, but they would eventually, if she had the desire to see any of them. She ducked under the scaffolding of a building under construction and found herself on a narrow sidewalk, jostled by passersby, all moving with purpose. Suddenly she noticed the figure of a jeans-clad man up ahead. He seemed to be inspecting the posters for movies, concerts, and other events that had been pasted onto the wooden siding surrounding the construction. She frowned. In a city the size of New York, it seemed nearly impossible that he'd find her again—the very same man who'd been on Toth's street, who had followed her at the UN. All at once he looked up and straight at her. There was an odd smile on his face and he seemed to be considering whether or not to approach her.

She didn't give him the opportunity. She turned on her heel and went back the way she'd come, turning right at the end of the construction site and found herself at a traffic light.

She crossed quickly when the traffic was stopped and hurried toward Forty-second Street, where she'd noticed a bus stop. A bus was approaching as she reached the stop and she got on, not sure where it would take her. There was no sight of the young man behind her, and she was so relieved that she convinced herself that she'd simply been imagining that he was the same person she'd thought was following her.

Happily, the bus was carrying her back toward where she'd started at Second Avenue, but she got off at Third Avenue and caught a bus heading uptown toward the Villa d'Este. It was time to get ready for Lady Margaret's charity party, in any case, and, more important, it was time to call Ted to tell him about her meeting with Gerald Toth, although there wasn't all that much to report except that she had the CDs that Toth wanted him to review.

Ted listened to her account of her meeting with Toth without comment and didn't even ask about her opinion of him. But he did sound concerned when she told him that she'd be carrying the CDs with the ERP program back to Connecticut.

"I'm a little nervous about that," she said. "He made them sound terribly valuable. I put them in the hotel safe."

"They are, and good for you."

"Mr. Toth also wanted me to tell you that three of four is missing and he'd send it promptly. Does that make any sense to you?"

"It does, as it turns out. But, Elizabeth, I doubt that anyone is going to steal the discs."

Betty wasn't so sure about that. She told him about the overheard conversation between Toth and an "Elliott" and how it seemed that the caller had stated some sort of threat. "Mr. Toth passed it off as an employee-looking-for-his-back-pay thing. I don't think so." Then she told him about the young man she'd seen at the UN, then outside Toth's building, and again later in Times Square.

"Call me at once if you see him again," Ted said seriously. "And try to get me a better description than 'ordinary, jeans, glasses.' It's probably Elliott Wolfson. I wonder what he's up to. Don't go anywhere alone."

"I promise," she said.

After all, she wouldn't exactly be alone tonight with Lady Margaret, Prince Paul, and all of New York society.

CHAPTER 14

BETTY DECIDED to enjoy the English tea in the lobby before getting ready for the evening. Once again the staff treated her like a VIP, and her personal young man even came around to remind her that Carolyn Sue Hoopes was expected back in New York on the weekend.

Betty paused to finish off the scone with strawberry preserves and clotted cream, then said, "Then I will have a chance to see her," but didn't admit that it would be more than merely seeing Carolyn Sue. She'd be meeting her for the first time. She must remember to ask Lady Margaret what the woman looked like so that she wouldn't embarrass herself by greeting the wrong person.

Tonight she would wear the new black dress that she'd bought for just such an occasion as the charity reception. She hoped that a long dress would be suitable, then decided she didn't care whether it was or not. After finishing her tea, she went back to her room to prepare.

The dress was perfect, but she hated her shoes. The dress would have to hide them. She also hated her hair and spent a long time pinning it up so that she looked more like an elegant society dowager than she ever imagined she could. She even applied a bit of her new makeup, and in the end she looked (she thought) quite presentable. Sid's pieces of jewelry were just the right touch, and she knew that no one would look down on her diamond earrings because people could see right away that they were the real thing.

When she was ready, she sat in a chair at the window that overlooked the street to watch the urban parade. It was just after the evening rush hour, but traffic still appeared to be heavy, although there weren't many pedestrians passing the hotel. Her coffee shop on the corner across the street was doing a thriving business.

Then she saw him. It was that young man again, directly across the street, watching the hotel entrance. She adjusted her thick glasses to get a good look at him, careful not to disturb the curtains and possibly alert him to her observation of him. There was really nothing to distinguish him. Uncombed, longish hair, glasses, and the same clothes she'd seen before. She couldn't tell how tall he was or his age. Nondescript, she'd call him. Then she noticed that he was lighting a pipe. Of course, now she remembered. The one thing that probably set him apart from thousands of other young men in the city. She wrote down the fact of the pipe on the back of the room-service menu. The next thing she noticed was that he was wearing a white T-shirt under his jacket. The jacket was unbuttoned, so she could see that the shirt had something written on it in red, but her poor old eyes weren't capable of reading the words. She made another note on the menu.

Then she frowned. It made her very nervous that he was trailing her. But who had sent him? As the sky began to darken, it was more difficult to see the man, but the white of his T-shirt remained visible for a long time. He wasn't going away.

When Lady Margaret called to say that she would be at the hotel in forty-five minutes, Betty wondered if he would still be standing there, watching her leave in Gerald Toth's town car. She hoped he would recognize it and believe that she was being taken to Toth's residence. Then he wouldn't try to follow them to the reception, which Margaret had told her was being held at a large art gallery uptown.

She only had her black suede coat, which she hoped wasn't too shabby for the grand event. Then she told herself that she was getting rather vain in her old age without yet having mixed with the upper classes. She went down to the lobby and was disappointed not to see her personal young man behind the front desk. She supposed the hotel must give him time off to do things other than attend to her. She boldly chose to stand outside near the doorman, almost directly across from her watcher. Yes, he was still there, and he was watching, but he drew back into the shadows of the building.

Betty didn't think twice. When there was a gap in the traffic, she marched across the street and confronted him.

"Young man, I must ask you why you are following me around the city."

"I'm not following you. I'm just waiting for a friend."

"And have you also been waiting for him in the United Nations gardens, Times Square, and on the street where Gerald Toth lives?"

"Give me a break, lady. Somebody asked me to keep track of you."

"And who would that be?" If he said Gerald Toth, she would be enraged.

"It's this woman I know." He was mumbling and his pipe had gone out, but he didn't relight it. "We're kind of business partners, and she lost something important. She thought maybe you could . . . lead me to it."

"I've found nothing, have nothing that belongs to your business partner, so I wish you'd stop trailing me. I assume you are Elliott." She heard an intake of breath. She'd guessed right. He was probably the person who had called to threaten Toth when she was meeting with him at his apartment. Then she saw Gerald Toth's car pull up in front of the hotel. "I have to leave now. If you wish to discuss this further, I'll meet you in that coffee shop on the corner tomorrow around nine."

The young man nodded—rather reluctantly, she noticed—and Betty recrossed the street to the car, to be handed in by the doorman. Margaret looked glamorous, and Betty was pleased to see that she was also wearing a long dress, this one in shades of pink. On the other side of her was a terribly good-looking young man with a straight nose and black hair and brows.

"Elizabeth, let me introduce Prince Paul Castrocani. Paul, this is Elizabeth Trenka from Connecticut who has some business in the city."

Betty put out her hand and Prince Paul brushed his lips across it with a gallantry she had never experienced. A prince!

"Delighted to meet you," he said. He had or affected a slight accent. "Margaret has spoken of you with warmth and tells me you know my mother."

"Well, not . . ." She had other things to think about and managed to glimpse her watcher quickly walking away from his post toward the avenue.

"Margaret, could you ask the driver to take a . . . a slightly circuitous route to wherever we're going?" she asked. "Someone seems to be following me. I'll explain . . ."

Margaret looked at her oddly, but said, "Edwards, don't take the direct route to the gallery." The car crossed Second Avenue and went on to First Avenue, where it turned uptown.

"All right," Margaret said. "Explain."

"A man has been following me today, and just now he was across the street, watching the hotel. I went over and spoke to him but got little satisfaction. I was hoping that he wouldn't try to follow us to the reception."

"Following you? Whatever for? Do you know him?"

"I don't, but I imagine it must have something to do with my business with Mr. Toth or perhaps Mr. Beame. I saw him near Mr. Toth's building after I left my meeting today. I went to Times Square to have a look at it and he was there, too."

"Miss Trenka, this could be serious!" Paul said. "There are many insane people on the streets of New York."

"Paul's right," Margaret said. "Perhaps we should consult with Gerald and see if he has enemies who might have fastened on to Miss Trenka because she visited him."

"I don't want to involve him," Betty said faintly, but it seemed to her that Margaret spoke with a determination that wouldn't be deflected easily.

"We'll worry about it tomorrow," Margaret said. "Surely he can't know that we are going to this particular gallery this evening." The car had turned west and was now traveling along a cross street, slowing, and turning onto an avenue, where a modern building with big glass windows ablaze with light was welcoming a stream of limos and town cars. Women in gowns and furs and men in evening dress were moving slowly up a broad flight of stairs and entering through a wide door. Their driver slipped in between two cars that had just dispensed their occupants and stopped exactly in front of the building.

"I hope you won't think this too tedious," Margaret said. "And you might find it fun to see how the so-called better classes amuse themselves."

"I will find it tedious," Paul said, "since Georgina is away for two weeks. She is so good at these affairs and doesn't require me to converse with tiresome women who believe that I would be the ideal match for their unattractive daughters with large trust funds."

As they got out of the car, Margaret whispered to Betty, "Georgina is his fiancée." It was rather like having a really close friend who understood that Betty would not be familiar with a name. Aloud she said, "Paul, darling, you know you've always been attracted to large trust funds, no matter what the girl looks like."

"I have my standards," Paul said, and took Betty's arm to guide her up the steps.

The foyer was thronged with chattering women in beautiful clothes and well-groomed men who were greeting friends. Paul took Betty's and Margaret's coats and left them with an attendant.

Betty gazed at the spectacle. "Why, they all look the same."

"Do you think so?" Margaret looked at the people, most of whom she knew from countless similar evenings. "I believe you're right." The hair, the style of the gowns, even the gowns' colors—mostly black, with a few daring reds—were the same. The women were painfully thin, although in a way different from Brunetta's skeletal shape. For one thing, one tended to forget the bones because her face was so lovely. The men, of course, were perfectly barbered and wore the latest Armani tuxedos. A stream of people moved slowly toward a big room at the top of another flight of stairs. When they reached the top, Betty saw young and attractive uniformed waiters and waitresses carrying trays with glasses of wine and platters of tiny hors d'oeuvres among the guests. No one seemed to eat much, but the sound of conversation was loud and shrill.

"There doesn't seem to be any volume control," Betty said, "but the hired help is pleasant to look at."

"Aspiring actors and actresses," Margaret said. "They have to earn a living somehow."

Paul was immediately surrounded by a bevy of women of all ages, and Betty saw him nod and smile at each one.

Several women approached Margaret. They were thin, had nice jewels, and had such tight skin on their faces that Betty was certain they had had face-lifts. "Darling Margaret, it's been ages . . ." This woman appeared to kiss the air around each of Margaret's cheeks, taking care not to touch her lest either one's makeup and hair be damaged.

"Candy, please meet my good friend, Elizabeth Trenka—"

"Trenka? Trenka?" The woman seemed to be leafing through a mental Rolodex. "Of course! The Prague Trenkas! I've been looking forward to meeting you at last. We did a lovely tour of Prague last year. Are your people arranging to get back the property those Communists took from your dear father? I was so distressed to hear that he had died in that dreadful hunting accident. The count was such a divine man. So amusing."

"I . . ." Betty was at a loss.

Margaret, like the best friend she was fast becoming, quickly stepped in. "There has been no resolution as yet, according to Elizabeth. These things take time. Ah, there's Terry Thompson. I do want you to meet her, Elizabeth." She guided Betty away from Candy.

"She thinks—" Betty began.

"Don't trouble yourself to wonder what she thinks," Margaret said. "Candy fancies herself knowledgeable on all matters of European nobility. If there was a count with your name, well, perhaps he actually was somehow distantly related. You've moved into the rarefied circle of people with a possible title, and soon everyone will know it because Candy is a terrible gossip. But if anyone asks how you should be addressed, I suggest you modestly say that in America you prefer to be called Miss Trenka and say no more. Did your father die, by the way?"

"Years ago," Betty said. "He worked in a factory. The only hunting he ever did was to get the gophers out of the garden in the back of the house."

"Then if people ask about him, say something like 'It was for the best.' Eyes downcast, a touch of sorrow. Nobody will pry if they think you're grieving. And questions about the repossession of the Trenka estates can be answered with just what I said. 'These things take time.' Think you can handle it?"

"Certainly. But it's such a sham."

"Don't you suppose everyone here is at least partly a sham? Well, they are. It may not have anything to do with a title or estates, although fake titles do abound, but bodies and faces have been reconfigured, hair color changed, husbands and wives exchanged for newer models, business deals have tested the law, people have been paid off. The dresses aren't all designer originals, the furs were bought at discount and the furrier may not have been strictly honest. I suppose . . ." Margaret looked around the gallery whose walls were hung with massive nudes. "I suppose the one thing here that isn't a sham is the art." She sipped her wine. "And the wine is a rather good one. Come along and meet Terry. She's a jolly person. Not heavily into sham, although she really can't decide on a hair color. There she is."

Betty was introduced to a somewhat formidable

lady who had chosen a deep black for tonight's hair color and her hair was styled in a youthful pageboy that didn't quite suit her.

"Candy was just saying to me that Miss Trenka is—" Terry said, but Margaret put a finger to her lips as if to say, "She'd rather not talk about it." Terry changed the subject on cue. "Where are you stopping in New York? Or do you live here? That can't be it or I would have seen you before."

"I'm at the Villa d'Este," Betty said, "but I live in Connecticut. In retirement."

"Well, of course. After all you've been through in your homeland. I understand things are much better now. You speak English perfectly."

Betty met Margaret's eyes. "I was brought up speaking English," she said. "My late father insisted on it."

Margaret nodded her approval. "Terry darling, Elizabeth and I want to have a look at the paintings, if you'll excuse us."

"I'm sure we'll run into each other again at this do. Miss Trenka, if you're going to be spending much time in New York, perhaps you'll join one of my committees. We do so much good work for the unfortunate."

"I'm afraid I have a great many family responsibilities just now. Perhaps in the future. So nice to have met you," Betty said as Margaret guided her away.

"You were born for this," Margaret said. "People

will be gossiping about you before the sun rises again. Who is she really? What is she doing here? Did they get their money out of Czechoslovakia? I heard it's all in Swiss banks. Elizabeth, you're perfect."

"I don't think this is the type of world I would care to be a part of," Betty said. "I couldn't keep up the pretense. I live in retirement because I'm retired. I've never set foot in Prague, although I'd love to travel there, and the only language I ever heard was English, except for my grandmother, who used to curse in Czech and sing old folk songs to me."

"Never mind," Margaret said. "You don't have to be swallowed up by these people. But I warn you. You're certain to receive invitations before the week is out."

"Me? For what? From what sort of people?"

"Those who want to be the first with the catch of the day. Somebody's going to reminisce about the old count—your father, that is. You'll have a grand time if you keep up the pretense. They won't really know anything and you'll be seeing how the better class lives."

They strolled about the gallery, examining the paintings that Betty didn't much care for although she recognized the name of the artist and knew he was very famous, indeed. She was pleased not to see the young man who had been trailing her at the reception, but of course he would definitely be out of place there and would probably be expelled promptly if he dared to enter.

In due course, after Margaret had introduced Betty to a mind-boggling array of identical men and women, they encountered Paul again, who said wearily, "I hope we don't have to stay here much longer. These women make my hair ache. Shall I take you ladies somewhere for a meal? Those little crab-meat-in-puff-pastry-shell bites are not enough to sustain me."

"Let's do," Margaret said. "Someplace simple and hearty. A deli or a Chinese place. Do you like Chinese food, Elizabeth?"

"I can't say that I have the opportunity very often. East Moulton, Connecticut, doesn't have many such places, although when I lived upstate in Hartford we did make an attempt at chopstick dining now and then."

"Done!" Margaret said. "Fetch our coats, Paul. We'll meet you at the door."

He obediently went off to retrieve the coats, while Betty and Margaret said their good-byes to some of the people they'd met.

"What was this party in honor of?" Betty asked. "There didn't seem to be a purpose to it."

"Some organization is raising money to help find a cure for a distressing disease. I'm not sure which one. They decided to use the opening of the artist's show as the occasion for a reception. Money from the tickets will go to the charity, the artist has people with fat wallets looking at his paintings, many of which will be sold to those here tonight. The event will be written up in the newspapers, so the general public will become more aware of the disease and the need to cure it. Society will be seen as benevolent in seeking the cure. The people who are here will be mentioned in the press and their pictures will appear in important magazines, which will please them greatly. Everybody wins."

"I hate to say this since you were so kind to invite me, but it seems a rather shallow way to live."

Just then a flashbulb half blinded Betty, catching her and Margaret as they were about to descend the stairs.

"Now you may appear in *W* or *New York* magazine," Margaret said. "And you're right. It is somewhat shallow. I'm trying to find a purpose for my life that doesn't include much of this sort of thing."

"Odd that you should say that," Betty said. "I'm trying to do the same thing."

CHAPTER 15

THEY FOUND a Chinese restaurant nearby, with Formica tabletops and paper napkins, two golden dragons decorating the walls. The waiter put a stainless-steel pot of tea and chopsticks packaged in red paper on the table and handed them huge menus.

"Anything you don't eat?" Margaret asked.

"I'm generally grateful for any food I don't have to cook myself," Betty said as she scanned the menu. "I seem to be doing very well in that department during my visit."

Paul said, "I recommend that you allow Margaret to choose the dishes. She and De Vere devote a lot of their time to things like Szechuan specialties and cases of murder."

Betty looked up and Paul grinned charmingly. "Just a little joke," he said.

"Sam De Vere is an occasional beau," Margaret said quickly. "He's a policeman."

Betty thought she understood the joke. "Then Mr. Toth is only one admirer among many."

"I told you that whatever was between Gerald and me is over," Margaret said. "I think he's still caught up in the magic of the Brunetta attraction. So unless she is arrested for shooting Gerald or me, I think he's going to stick with her until a more savory bit of decorative female turns up."

Margaret proceeded to order: steamed dumplings, spare ribs in black bean sauce, General Tso's chicken, beef with oyster sauce, a whole fried sea bass.

"It seems like quite a bit for three people," Betty said cautiously.

"We'll put all the dishes on the table and share," Margaret said. "Don't worry, if it seems like a lot of food, I'll take the leftovers home. I honestly enjoy a second go at Chinese."

"What did you think of the art, Miss Trenka?" Paul asked. "A bit heavy for my taste. The models, I mean. Although some of the paintings in my father's villa near Rome show voluptuous women, but that was the style of the Renaissance. Modern women tend to be so very thin. You'd think he'd paint what is reality."

"But people, aside from those at the reception tonight, tend to be very well nourished. Teenage girls may strive for the anorexic look, but most adults are sturdy enough, and that's reality," Betty said. "I really don't know much about art and am not even sure what I like. Conventional things. Flowers and nice scenes. Although I do intend to visit the Metropolitan Museum of Art to broaden my knowledge.

And, Lady Margaret, I am planning to see a new show tomorrow. *The Serpent's Tooth*."

"I've heard of it," Margaret said. "I'll be curious to hear how they handle *King Lear* with music. I imagine the fool will stop the show with his big number. I think I'll wait to hear what the critics have to say before I venture there."

Betty was glad she hadn't purchased a ticket for Lady Margaret.

The waiter brought their food. Betty attempted to eat with chopsticks and, with a little coaching from Margaret, managed quite well. Paul resorted to a fork, and told tales of his father, Prince Aldo, and listed his mother's recent expensive acquisitions. "My mother likes owning Things," he said. "Doesn't matter what they are—houses, horses, clothes, jewels, anything at all. Then she has to find a place to put everything, and that usually means adding a wing to her house or buying another building."

Betty couldn't imagine anyone like Carolyn Sue but was eager to get a look at her. "Someone at the hotel said that she was returning to New York this weekend," Betty said. "I'd like to meet her."

"You will," Margaret said. "I'll see to it. And don't listen to Paul. Carolyn Sue can afford to buy anything she wants and she has lovely taste, so whatever she acquires is usually perfect. Paul would just prefer that she wrote the checks to him rather than to Neiman Marcus, Bergdorf's, and Harry Winston."

"I did appreciate it when she purchased Pratesi

linens for my apartment," Paul said, "but I could have gotten along with Martha Stewart's Kmart sheets and enjoyed the difference in price in more entertaining ways."

"Never mind, darling Paul. One day you'll inherit that Raphael painting in your father's villa and have it auctioned off by Christie's or Sotheby's for millions."

"If he doesn't do so first." Paul was even glummer now.

"Paul yearns for the life of luxury and leisure he once lived, Elizabeth. We go through this almost every time we meet. Are you enjoying the meal?"

"The food is delicious," Betty said, "although I haven't quite gotten the hang of chopsticks."

Paul waved his fork and grinned. Apparently he was quickly able to forget his lack of funds and his mother's excess of them. "Forks are the answer. And please, Miss Trenka, don't think that I am solely concerned with money. I have friends, I like pretty women, and if I wanted to, I could change my name and still be welcome in society."

"I'm not sure changing one's name makes everything right," Betty said. "There was a story in the news in Connecticut a while back. A young woman was found drowned at some little beach resort on the coast. The police suspected foul play, and it turned out they were right. I don't think they ever found out who did it, but they had a difficult time locating her family because she'd changed her name to . . ."

"What is it, Elizabeth?"

"She had some ordinary name, Janet or Jane, but she changed it to Xaviera." Betty frowned.

"But that's the name of Gerald's company," Margaret said. "Oh, it's ridiculous. Gerald doesn't go around murdering women at the seashore who dare to call themselves by the name of his company. It has to be a coincidence. I don't remember him ever saying that he's even been to Connecticut in his life."

"Of course there's no connection," Betty said. "It's just that I only remembered her name now."

They finished their dinner, the waiter packed up the leftovers, and they went out to find Gerald Toth's car patiently awaiting them. Betty looked around the street but didn't see the young man in jeans anywhere about. She hoped she wouldn't find him lurking across from the hotel.

"Can I take you somewhere tomorrow, Elizabeth?" Margaret asked.

"I plan to visit a museum or two," Betty said, "then go to the theater in the evening. I'm sure you have your own affairs to attend to. I can manage perfectly well, though you've been so kind."

"Be sure to ring me on Friday to report on *Lear*. I can't imagine what it will be like. And do consult me about the invitations I promised you'd be receiving. Some of them might be for entertaining events."

"Surely no one will believe that I am related to European nobility."

"People in New York are ready to believe anything," Paul said, "and I'm sure those at the reception took close note of your diamonds. I noticed myself, but I have had much experience in appreciating precious gems, thanks to my mother."

The aroma of the Chinese food in a plastic bag at Margaret's feet filled the town car as they made their way downtown. No shadowy figures were lurking in doorways around the hotel as Betty was welcomed by the doorman and then disappeared inside.

"Xaviera is not a common name," Margaret said to Paul as they drove away. "I wonder if the dead woman Elizabeth mentioned was known to Gerald. The lost love everyone says he named his company for. If she's the one, he's now on the other end of the gun." She told Paul about Brunetta's appearance at the restaurant the other night.

"Brunetta is quite well known for her passionate temper and her intense interest in establishing a sound financial footing. It may not be such a fortunate thing to possess outrageous amounts of money," Paul said. "Although I would choose the experience, just to see how it felt. Miss Trenka is quite a pleasant lady, isn't she?"

"I like her a lot. There's more substance to her than meets the eye, I think. I wonder what Gerald thinks of her."

What Gerald Toth was thinking just then was not about Elizabeth Trenka. The driver had reported to him where he had taken her, Margaret, and Prince

Paul and informed him when the Trenka woman was safely back at her hotel. That was all he needed to know. What Toth was seriously pondering was how to handle the continuing phone calls from Elliott, who was just a thief who wanted his payoff. But Elliott wasn't going to get a cent until Toth knew he could get away with releasing the ERP as his own product. He wasn't going to put a lot of money in the hands of the person Ivor Beame knew had handed over the ERP program to his competitor.

Then there was the other worry. Where was the missing CD? The program was so large, it had to be copied onto four discs. He knew there were four discs in the California set. So when did one go missing from the New York one? Almost no one came to his apartment. Certainly Sonny wouldn't have the faintest idea of what a CD was. Then he felt a sudden cold clutch of anxiety. Brunetta had been there a week or two ago before she went off on that weekend photo shoot, and she, who was circling around Ivor Beame "caregiving," would certainly know that software programs were stored on CDs.

At least Ted Kelso would recognize immediately that one was missing and that would tell him how much programming was needed to make the system work. But not to worry, Toth had the copy in California. He couldn't mention the missing disc to the programmers he had on staff at Xaviera, because they would be sure to gossip. And where was it? Perhaps Elliott was holding one disc for ransom, hoping that his payout would be bigger. But he wouldn't get a cent until the set of CDs was complete. Toth didn't have time to arrange for the duplicate set of discs to be retrieved in California and sent to him and then to Ted Kelso. Time was very important.

He intended to bring Elliott to his study and shake the truth from him if necessary. He'd have Sonny in the background as an added inducement.

Then he thought about poor Xaviera. How foolish of her to have gone off to be drowned. At first he had hoped that it was merely a coincidence of names, but then the police had tracked him down.

She'd been a beauty and should have had a career like Brunetta's, her face on every magazine cover. She even looked a bit like Brunetta except for the dark hair. But she preferred serious work. A few months in Xaviera's California offices doing routine tasks and then she was gone, only leaving the message that she'd come back to him. There was something important she needed to do. Then silence and, in the end, death. He'd thought about changing the company's name, but he'd wanted her to know where to find him. Besides, he'd spent a lot of advertising dollars to make the name world famous. No going back now. But somebody had that missing disc.

Gerald Toth sat up late watching television while Sonny dozed nearby in an easy chair.

Betty yawned, carefully put away her diamond

earrings and her long black dress, and retired for the night. Margaret and Paul found their separate homes, and the tide came in and filled the shallow pool among the rocks on a stretch of beach far up the Connecticut coast.

CHAPTER 16

TED SPENT his Tuesday and Wednesday evenings examining the disc he'd retrieved from Stan Thurlow. When he first put it into the CD drive of his computer and saw the lines of code appearing on his screen, he knew for certain what he had. The ERP program, although he had only part of it.

He scratched his head. How had the disc come to be in the possession of the dead woman? These discs certainly wouldn't have been left lying around so that anyone could pick them up. While there might be duplicate sets, even they would be locked away carefully. And if someone wanted to steal the discs, the whole set would be taken, and the thief wouldn't allow one to be separated from the others. Yet that appeared to be what had happened. Somehow it had gotten into the hands of the woman who had died. The thief's set of discs was worthless without it. And thus it was worthless to Gerald Toth as well. And the final question was, had the woman died because she had the disc?

Early on Thursday morning he called Betty to review the issue of the missing disc and the murder.

"Miss Trenka's room does not answer," the hotel operator told him. "Please hold for the front desk."

The man at the front desk said, "Miss Trenka went out just before nine. She mentioned she was meeting someone at the coffee shop across the street. Shall I have someone run across to fetch her?"

"No," Ted said, and left his name. "I'll try to reach her later."

Betty found an empty booth and sat facing the door. She wasn't certain that Elliott would appear. But he did, a few minutes after nine, looking as though he'd scarcely slept, and those were certainly the same clothes he'd been wearing the day before. She recognized the white T-shirt with the red lettering. He hesitated before he slid into the booth opposite her.

"What do you want?" he asked.

"I'm curious about a missing disc from a big computer program," Betty said.

Elliott slumped down in his seat. "It doesn't matter that it's missing, there are others. The only thing that matters is why it was taken. I think it was just to get me in trouble, because I'm the only person who had the complete set. I'm the one who took the program from Ivor Enterprises and handed it over to Gerald Toth at Xaviera."

"Was the set complete when you handed it over to Gerald Toth?"

"Yeah. He probably had a copy made."

"So someone stole it from him. Did you think I knew where it was? Is that why you've been following me?"

He shook his head. "I found out you were Ted Kelso's assistant and were coming here to wrap up his deal with Toth."

"Who knew? Who could have told you about me?" Toth knew, Ted knew, and of course Ivor Beame seemed to know everything about her. She was mystified. "Elliott, I don't know exactly what you imagine I'm here for, but I'm not an important person. I don't carry around valuable computer discs with me." But then she realized that of all the millions of people in New York City at the moment, she was the only one who actually knew where the missing disc was. Ted Kelso had it, courtesy of his friend Stan in Connecticut. Why, then, had Xaviera been killed? It must have been because she'd had the disc. She had been going to do something with it and damage someone's interests. Betty knew she needed to call Ted right away.

"Elliott, I have some appointments this morning. I'm afraid I can't stay any longer." Elliott quickly wolfed down the last piece of toast from his breakfast. The poor kid acted as though he was starving. "I'll take care of the check," Betty said.

"Thanks. I'd be doing okay if Toth paid me what he promised. I'll return the favor someday."

Betty hurried back to the hotel, where she was stopped by her friend at the front desk. "These are for you, Miss Trenka. We were just about to take them up to your room."

He handed her a stack of thick, creamy envelopes, some were pale blue or pale pink, all of them were addressed by hand in proper black ink. And all of them had her name on them. A couple even called her "The Honorable Elizabeth Trenka." None of them bore postage stamps, but when she turned them over, most of them had an engraved return address on the flap. Fifth Avenue, Park Avenue, Sutton Place . . . "What is all this?" Betty asked.

"Apparently you are socially in demand, Miss Trenka. They were all delivered by hand," the desk clerk said. "People do that because the post office is not always prompt in its deliveries, so a messenger is worth the money to some people."

"I had better ask Lady Margaret to help me sort them out," Betty said. "Please send up any others that arrive. I will be here for a time but will be going out later."

The chambermaid had already been there to re-make her bed and toss out some of the flowers in the arrangement that had begun to fade. The towels were fresh, and she could see the marks of the vacuum cleaner on the carpet. Even the soap she'd used had been replaced by a new wrapped bar.

She opened the envelope at the top of the pile and found a nice engraved card inviting her to dine that evening with people she didn't know, in honor of a person she also did not know.

She put the invitations aside to call Ted, then recounted to him exactly what Elliott had told her, especially the fact that someone had known she was coming to New York to meet with Toth and told Elliott. "I'd say Ivor Beame," Betty said. "He knew everything about me when I saw him on Tuesday."

"But Elliott no longer works for him in any capacity. If it were me, I wouldn't even speak to him."

"I feel a little sorry for poor Elliott. Here he went to all that trouble to steal something really big and Toth won't pay him what was promised. I guess that says something about Gerald Toth. He can't be trusted to pay his debts. Ted, are you really going ahead with this project? There are crimes involved— theft and murder—and I wouldn't want any harm to come to you, either from these people who seem to want that disc so much or those who killed. Tell me, if other copies of the program exist, why is this one disc so important?"

"It's a later version, Version Two," Ted said. "I found 'v.2' in tiny letters on the disc, right below 'III/IV.' Some programmer, probably Elliott, must have done some refinements after the basic program was completed. Toth got Version One, and had a copy made, but needs Version Two as well. I think you've mostly done your job. What are you doing for the rest of your visit?"

Betty looked at the pile of envelopes on the table next to the bed. "I am, according to the front desk clerk, socially in demand. I have a pile of invitations that should keep me entertained and fed for weeks."

"Where did they come from?"

"People seem to think I am someone I'm not. I guess that's the way New York works. I'm looking forward to going home. Things are simpler in East Moulton."

She rang Margaret, who burst into laughter when Betty reported her sudden social prominence. "I told you it would happen. Look through them quickly and I'll tell you which ones might be fun."

"I certainly will go nowhere tonight. My theater ticket was far too expensive to toss away. But here's one for Friday from Mrs. Draper Burns, a dinner dance in honor of her daughter's birthday."

"No, no," Margaret said. "Ernestine is the woman who got that huge divorce settlement and demanded all kinds of money to support the child who can't be more than six. You don't want to attend a child's birthday party that will be marked by wretched excess. I shouldn't imagine the little girl would be allowed to stay up to enjoy the dancing. What else?"

"On Saturday another dinner—no dancing promised—at River House in honor of somebody I don't recognize." Betty read off the name.

"That might be fun. Very grand people will be there. In fact, I have an invitation to that do myself, and if Carolyn Sue is back in time, she'll certainly be on the guest list. What do you say we make an appearance?"

"I will let you guide me, Margaret."

"Then I'll ring up Biffie and accept for both of us. What else?"

"All sorts of things, but, Margaret, I really don't want to attend a lot of social affairs. I'm going home on Sunday after all. I really don't have the clothes to deck myself out properly for these things, and I don't want to buy more."

"Fine. You're in charge. You'll have to call them all to decline, which might be a chore. I have it! Take them down to the concierge and have him telephone them all to decline. Have him say that you've been called out of the city on family business. They'll like that, and the concierge will be delighted to be ringing up all the biggest names in social New York. They tend to be quite the snobs. There's just Friday to worry about. Any more Friday invitations?"

"Your friend Terry Thompson has asked me around for cocktails on Friday. She seemed like a nice woman. At least she wasn't so skinny she was transparent."

"Terry always has pleasant little gatherings. I don't know that I'll be there, however. Sam De Vere insists that I spend the evening with him."

"Good," Betty said. "Is Gerald Toth likely to be there? The more I see of him, the less I think of him."

"I don't think he's one of Terry's pets. Although he's rich enough, he's not really high enough up on the society food chain to suit Terry, so I doubt that he'll be there. All right, your social calendar is arranged. You're not still being pursued, are you?"

"I took the boy to breakfast this morning and found out a bit more. I think he's confused about what he should do, but I find that most amateur criminals aren't always intelligent about their choices. Right now I think I'll go to the Metropolitan Museum of Art and look at the mummies."

"Do you need a car?"

"I'm going to try the subway," Betty said. "It seems like something one should do when in New York."

CHAPTER 17

*B*ETTY EXAMINED her subway map and thought she had it firmly in mind. If she walked a few short blocks to Lexington Avenue, she could catch a local train that would take her up to Seventy-seventh Street. Then she'd walk over to Fifth Avenue and up to Eighty-second and she'd be at the museum. She'd spend a few hours there, then take a bus or a taxi back to her hotel, get ready for the theater, and another day would be over. Nothing to it.

The concierge was delighted to take care of Miss Trenka's pile of invitations and quite understood her dilemma: so many invitations, so little time, and just to be sure everything was handled properly, Betty added, "I do want to be free for Mrs. Hoopes if she gets back before I leave."

It probably wasn't necessary. Everyone at the hotel knew she was Carolyn Sue's chum, and Lady Margaret's as well, and the invitations were simply icing on the cake. She tipped the concierge generously, thankful that that task was not in her hands, and headed out for a cultural adventure, taking time only to call the nursing home to check in with Sid. She knew some people scoffed at her devotion to the ailing man, and just for a moment she thought of Brunetta caring for Ivor Beame. Gerald had said that Brunetta tried to shoot him because of Margaret, but as Betty strolled toward Lexington Avenue, she wondered. What if Brunetta had been protecting Ivor or punishing the man who had accepted Ivor's stolen property?

She stopped in the middle of the sidewalk. If Elliott knew all about her and had been told by a nameless "someone," Betty was convinced that that someone was Brunetta, who could have been told about her by Ivor.

Betty missed the town car, and that's when she knew that she had been totally spoiled by this trip. Here she was, reduced to the subway. She found the entrance at Fifty-first Street and descended the steps. The walls were damp and the stairs weren't exactly clean. She saw one huddle of humanity lying on cardboard and covered with a grimy brown coat. She knew it was a person, because a sneakered foot extended beyond the coat. After she had bought a token and passed through the turnstile, she looked at the signs. There were a few other people in the station, but no one at all threatening. Teenage girls, a businessman or two. Just then an express train zipped through the station without stopping and she became disoriented. Surely she should be traveling uptown, but the sign seemed to indicate that this was the downtown track. How to get to the other side? She approached the token seller's booth and stopped.

Surely that wasn't Brunetta just entering the station. The woman appeared to be blond and she was certainly thin, but she was wearing a scarf around her head and big dark glasses. She carried a huge leather satchel over her shoulder. She ignored Betty and went to sit on a bench next to one of the businessmen. Betty took a seat some distance from her.

This was too much of a coincidence. What would Brunetta be doing in the very subway station that Betty had chosen? The wrong subway station for that matter. She decided she'd better ask for directions. Just as she approached the token booth again, she heard a train coming into the station. Perhaps if she got on board and rode it, even in the wrong direction, she could get out at Grand Central and take another train back uptown to the museum.

It was the local train and it slowed to a stop. The doors opened and a few people got out. Keeping an eye on Brunetta, who didn't seem to be moving, Betty stepped into the car. She found a seat and then, just before the doors closed, she saw Brunetta glide into the car and take a seat at the far end facing her. She had an odd little smile on her face, as though she was feeling smugly clever. Someone had said that Brunetta wasn't clever at all, but Betty wondered if she was driven by her attachments, if not to Ivor Beame himself then at least to his money. She hoped Brunetta had left her little gun at home.

The two women watched each other out of the corners of their eyes. At Grand Central quite a large number of people got on, filling the seats, but the crush was not too bad. Betty realized that she should have gotten out there, but it was too late now. The train was moving again.

The next time she looked, Brunetta had found a seat closer to Betty. She had taken the scarf off her head and had draped it around her shoulders. It was Brunetta all right, and now she was watching Betty closely. Betty stood up as though she was about to get off the train at the next stop, wherever that might be. Worst case, she would go to the street and hail a taxi. Or perhaps Brunetta would get off and Betty could stay on to the next stop. First Elliott and now Brunetta going to great lengths to trail her, when she had nothing to be trailed about.

The train slowed and Brunetta stood up, moving in Betty's direction. The sign in the station meant nothing to Betty, and she didn't know what kind of neighborhood she would be facing if she got off now. She stayed on the train and eventually saw the signs for Astor Place and then Spring Street in the next stations. Finally the train pulled into Canal Street. That was a name she recognized. Chinatown. In fact, at dinner the other night both Prince Paul and Margaret had extolled the glories of Chinatown cuisine. Betty edged casually so as to be in place in front of the doors when they opened, and as soon as they did, she darted out into the dark, murky station. There were a lot of Chinese women with loaded shopping carts and plastic grocery-store bags who pushed their way onto the train, delaying Brunetta's exit. Betty dashed toward the token booth and the stairs to the street.

She was panting when she reached the top of the stairs and she looked around in confusion. This was nothing like the New York she'd been seeing. Low tenementlike buildings with lines of laundry were above her and a constant traffic jam of cars trying to move through impossibly narrow streets. The shops displayed Oriental trinkets on sidewalk tables, and every other shop seemed to be a restaurant. There were grocery and produce stores and baskets of fish and blue crabs.

Betty looked around but saw no sign of Brunetta. Maybe she had given up on her silly quest.

This was a long way from the mummies at the Met, but as Betty strolled the streets, she found the bustling scene interesting. She didn't recognize the piles of strange fruits and vegetables; she marveled at the roasted ducks and ribs hanging in shop windows. One little street-corner place displayed an array of embroidered slippers, porcelain teapots and rice bowls, and bundles of incense. She ventured into one of the grocery stores and watched the determined, jostling shoppers filling their carts with twenty-pound bags of rice and gallons of soy sauce.

She wandered the narrow streets, looking back now and then. No Brunetta in sight. Finally she turned down a narrow street, where the walls of the buildings leaned inward, almost touching. More shops, several with signs reading "No firework." The street was almost empty of pedestrians and even the cars seemed to avoid it.

It must have been a firecracker that startled her, a *pop pop* sound in the nearly silent street. Betty turned quickly and glimpsed Brunetta retreating down another side street.

Had she been shooting at Betty with that little gun of hers? Why? Betty's heart was beating fast and she sought a street crowded with cars. No taxis to be seen, but she thought the subway entrance was just down the street to her left, not that she wanted to be trapped again on a subway car with a demented high-fashion model. She walked past the subway station until she reached a group of official-looking buildings. Government offices, she decided. They all had the same look. There she did spot a taxi or two, but all of them were occupied. Finally an empty cab appeared and she flagged it down. She told the driver where she wanted to go, and as they moved away, Betty glimpsed Brunetta standing on a curb, stuffing something into her shoulder satchel. She didn't seem to notice Betty, who hunched down in the cab seat until they had passed her.

It took a while and quite a few dollars to return

her to the hotel. She definitely needed a lie-down before the theater. First she called Gerald Toth.

"It's Elizabeth Trenka. I'm sorry to trouble you, but I wonder if you could tell me why your model girlfriend would have been following me today."

"Bru? I can't imagine. She did telephone me today to say that she was straightening out her life. Didn't know what she meant, except that she made it clear that I wasn't a part of that straightening. Be careful of her, Miss Trenka. I'm convinced she's dangerous, although she can't be said to think logically."

"Did she know your friend Xaviera?"

There was a long pause. "Why do you ask?"

"Miss Trumbull seems to be enamored of violence. I was just wondering if she had some reason to do violence to your Xaviera."

"I won't listen to this," Toth said. "Good-bye, Miss Trenka."

Betty looked for a moment at the silent phone. Then she stretched out on the bed and closed her eyes. She awoke at six, dressed for the theater, and stopped for a dish of ice cream at the coffee shop. Then she found a cab to take her to the theater, where she arrived a few moments before the curtain went up.

Betty quickly decided that a musical version of *King Lear* was about the stupidest idea anyone had ever had. The sets were spectacular and moved and changed on cue. The performers threw their hearts into their roles, and indeed Goneril had a touching song in the first act: "I love you more than [words] can wield the matter,/Dearer than eyesight, space and liberty,/Beyond what can be valued, rich or rare,/No less than life, with grace, health, beauty, honor . . ." The audience ate it up, but Betty didn't think it would give "Some Enchanted Evening" a run for its money.

They all died in the end as expected, and a scrim with a toothed serpent ended the play. The audience demanded many curtain calls, but Betty was doubtful. The thing she took away with her was the picture of young women, sisters bound together in tragedy, and an old man, but she wondered if music and *Lear* were quite the right combination.

There were no taxis available, so she took the buses she'd taken earlier during her visit to get back to the hotel. She had a slight headache and slept late into the morning.

Margaret's call awakened her. "You've made the columns, Elizabeth. Have them bring you the tabloids and look at Poppy Dill's 'Social Scene' column. 'Doyenne of Prague society, Elizabeth Trenka, is gracing our city for a few days and is being feted and entertained left and right,'" Margaret read.

"What nonsense," Betty said. "Doyenne, indeed. I don't even know what it means." But she would find a paper to take home to Connecticut to show Molly.

"How was the show?"

"More nonsense. I'm no critic, of course, and

everyone seemed to try very hard, but, well . . . I'd like to see the reviews when it opens. I can't imagine that people will take *King Lear* set to music seriously, although the actor who played Lear was quite affecting. He had a big number in the first act that quite captured the spirit of the play. You know, 'How sharper than a serpent's tooth it is/To have a thankless child!' Ah, Margaret. Now I have Brunetta trailing me, and I think she may have shot at me yesterday."

"Good heavens! What do you have to do with her?"

"I suppose she thinks I know things I don't know. She seems to enjoy shooting at people, though. Like a child with a new and dangerous toy who uses it to get her way."

"Dangerous," Margaret said slowly, "but not a thankless child. Elizabeth, remember that girlfriend of Gerald's who was killed in Connecticut? She supposedly did some harm to Ivor Beame, did she not? And Brunetta . . ."

". . . was more of an age to be his child than his bride. Margaret! You don't suppose that Brunetta set out with her dangerous toy to avenge Ivor."

"Xaviera wasn't shot."

"I asked Mr. Toth just a short time ago whether Brunetta had a reason to harm Xaviera."

"And he said?"

"He just hung up the phone," Betty said. "I think I ought to call Ted Kelso again and have him contact our resident state trooper in East Moulton. He could have people start checking on Brunetta's whereabouts when Xaviera was drowned."

"I could ask Sam De Vere tonight what we ought to do. It's a fairly flimsy assumption on our part. Mere suspicion because of the unusual circumstances of the people involved. And you won't have any problem getting to Terry's cocktail hour tonight, will you?"

"Of course not. I've mastered the subway and the bus system and I know how to hail a cab. Of course, I'll miss my town car, but a doyenne can handle anything. Margaret, I don't believe there's much society to speak of in Prague, do you?"

Betty called Ted to share the conclusions she and Margaret had reached about Brunetta.

"Very thin," Ted said.

"But so is Brunetta."

"I'll speak to somebody. Maybe Stan can consult with his own cop in Redding's Point. They probably have evidence of something they haven't shared with him, and it might give them a direction to pursue. I'm pretty sure now that the three-of-four disc is the key. Someone—Xaviera or that Elliott—removed it from a set that was handed over to Toth and was holding it hostage for a bigger payoff."

"That can't be right. Toth said he had burned a duplicate and left it in California, so he must have had a complete set of CDs at one time."

"I told you that the set the missing disc came from

was a later version. Elliott was probably planning to ask for more money for the new version, and to be sure he got it, he handed over a set with one disc missing. Or else Xaviera extracted disc three and planned to give it to her old love, Gerald Toth. Brunetta decided to retrieve it and failed.

"I'll let you know what comes of this," Ted said. "I can tell you, though, that just looking at the disc I have, I judge the code to be Elliott's work. So I have no doubt that it was work done while Elliott was employed by Ivor Enterprises and is definitely stolen."

"Are you going to proceed with working for Toth?"

"Not a chance," Ted said.

CHAPTER 18

BETTY WONDERED if she was up for a cocktail party, especially since she had no shoes to wear that seemed appropriate. She regretted her vanity but consulted the concierge, who suggested she try Bloomingdale's.

"Unless madam wishes to visit one of the designer shops . . . Prada, Gucci, Fendi. But if you have limited time, Bloomingdale's has several shoe departments." He kindly did not suggest that if her budget was also limited, the shops he mentioned were probably out of her league. She knew quite well what designer shoes cost from her reading of the "Fashions of the Times" section of the Sunday *New York Times*.

She hustled over to Third Avenue and plunged into the uncontrolled shopping swirl at the big beige department store. Although it was a Friday afternoon, dedicated shoppers were out in force. Betty roamed around for a while, dodging perfume-spraying saleswomen until she found an information desk that directed her upward to a shoe salon. A bored young thing heard her requirements: low heels, black, comfortable, suitable for a festive occasion. The salesclerk almost, but not quite, sneered at Betty's own well-worn pumps and brought out a pile of boxes. It didn't take Betty long to choose a pair of elegant black suede flats, decorated with a few green and blue stones. She paid the rather high price and resisted the urge to wander through the store to look at the array of clothes, handbags, jewelry, and cosmetics that were for sale. She reminded herself that she claimed not to be a dedicated shopper. Still, in a moment of weakness, she spotted a rack of glittery dresses and paused for a look. She was captivated by a deep purple outfit with a long straight skirt and a simple matching blouse topped with a gauzy jacket in a slightly lighter shade of purple, embroidered with swirls of silver. For almost the first time in her life, she had found something she felt she must have. So she guiltily paid the price and fled before any further and expensive enticements caught her eye.

Back in her hotel room, which was beginning to feel like home, she donned her green satin jacket, a simple skirt, and her new shoes, which embraced her feet as if they had been made especially for her. Then she set out for Terry Thompson's apartment, where she was greeted warmly by Terry, who introduced her to another set of women with no body fat to speak of. All of them had read Poppy Dill's "Social Scene" column, so everyone knew who she was. Or thought they did.

She was able to make pleasant conversation about *The Serpent's Tooth,* which no one had yet seen, but apparently her reservations about the musical didn't sway them from their determination to see it the very first chance they had. She thought perhaps they were simply trying to get on her good side. There were one or two awkward moments when people brought up her "late father" and the vast Trenka estates lost to the Communists, but Betty worked her way through the discussion with ease, even remarking to one that her father's tragic hunting accident had been entirely his fault. "He never knew one end of a gun from the other" was what she said, and that was quite true. Pop had always been opposed to guns and refused to have one in the house. Besides, he had said, if the Nazis ever invaded America and got to his little corner of Connecticut, no gun of his was going to be able to stop them.

One woman with an especially large diamond ring and very expensive clothes complained loudly to Betty about the fact that her daughter had become engaged to a wealthy, prominent broker. "He is far too old for her. Such a waste of youth and beauty, but she won't hear a word against him. She says he has so much to give her, and she will defend him with her life. These girls don't know what the world is all about. Since she's my daughter, she knows it's all about money, so it may work out."

Betty thought again about Brunetta and Ivor Beame. Money, marriage, thankless children. The

stolen disc wasn't important. What had been important to Brunetta was defending Ivor Beame's resources, which she hoped would become hers.

"I'm sure your daughter thinks she knows what
she's doing," Betty said. "And I don't know that parents have any way of stopping children from making
a mistake, if that's what it is. You'll feel more peaceful if you let nature take its course. The man could be
poor and without prospects."

"You want me to look on the bright side," the
woman said. "You're a wise woman, your . . .
your . . ." She seemed to be fumbling for the correct
title for Betty, who hoped she wouldn't come up with
"your majesty."

"Please call me Elizabeth," she said, and the
woman seemed thrilled to be on a first-name basis
with an important person. Betty never learned the
woman's name.

She didn't stay long at the cocktail party, because she had run out of ways to sidestep questions
about her background. But she did promise Terry
Thompson that she would certainly join one of her
committees if she decided to move to New York permanently.

On Saturday, she finally managed to reach the
Metropolitan Museum of Art and spent long hours
inspecting the mummies and the massive statues of
Egyptian gods and pharoahs. She looked at some gal-
leries containing Renaissance paintings and wondered if Prince Paul's father really had similar works

on his walls in his villa near Rome. Maybe she'd visit him someday, after she'd stopped at Priam's Priory to meet Lady Margaret's brother, the earl.

When she returned to the Villa d'Este, she found a commotion in the lobby. A pile of Vuitton suitcases were in front of the reception desk, a flurry of hotel staff was tripping over one another, and standing in the middle of it all was a blindingly blond woman whose jewels lit up the lobby as she directed people to do her bidding. The drawl was unmistakable. It could be no one but Carolyn Sue Hoopes. Betty hung back near the entrance, for even if she could identify Carolyn Sue, there was no way Carolyn Sue would know who she was. She didn't want to be embarrassed before all the nice people who had assumed so many things about her.

Then her personal young man approached. "I told Mrs. Hoopes that you'd only just returned, and she's eager to see you."

"Now? I mean . . ."

Then without warning Betty was embraced by the woman, who crushed her face to Betty's cheek. "Why, Miz Trenka, honey, I was worryin' that I'd miss you, but the spa did wonders for me. They pummeled and prodded and I don't know what-all, until I was feelin' like a kid of sixteen. I was talkin' to Margaret on the way in from the airport, and she says we're goin' to some godawful dinner tonight. I hope I have the energy to get through it."

Betty didn't doubt that Mrs. Hoopes had energy to burn.

"I have a car to take us, so don't you worry about that. Eight o'clock. Ah, here's my boy come to see his old mother!"

Prince Paul kissed his mother on both cheeks and nodded to Betty. He said softly, "I need to remind her about my allowance check."

Mother and son were hustled away to the elevator by a pack of bellmen carrying Carolyn Sue's bags. Betty waited until they were gone, then went to her own room. There was a message for her from Ted, and she called him back.

"Very clever of you to hit on Brunetta," he said. "It appears that she was away from New York on a modeling assignment the weekend that Xaviera died and went missing from the shoot one foggy evening. The people she was working with remember seeing her with a dark-haired woman. They went off somewhere together, but Brunetta came back alone."

"I didn't know Brunetta and Xaviera knew each other."

"They were both involved with Ivor Beame in one way or another. Maybe even rivals for his affection— or his money. And they were both involved with Toth."

For a moment Betty felt sorry for Gerald Toth. His current love appeared to have murdered his former one. Then she said, "But Xaviera had the disc."

"It's possible she was planning to demand money from Beame for the return of the disc. Or else she'd turn it over to Toth. When are you coming back to East Moulton?"

"Tomorrow," Betty said, "and it's not soon enough. You're right. The social ramble can be very tiring. I have one more event tonight, and then it's on to the train and home. I'll take the noon train, which should get me there a bit after one-thirty."

"I'll be at the station," Ted said. "And, Elizabeth, you've done a good job under challenging circumstances. You accomplished what you set out to do."

Almost Sister Rita's words in the letter that now seemed to have been received so long ago. And by a different person almost. Today Elizabeth Trenka was not merely a retired businesswoman living quietly in Connecticut but a habitué of elegant restaurants, a shopper at legendary department stores, the descendant of Czech nobility—a veritable party girl!

CHAPTER 19

BETTY WOULDN'T quite admit to herself that she'd bought the purple outfit because she wanted to look especially nice at the dinner party with Carolyn Sue and Margaret. Then she finally nodded to herself and owned up to the fact that she liked being thought of as one of the better classes of people and clothes do make a difference. She wondered if she'd become so spoiled by New York that she'd have trouble settling back into her routineless life in East Moulton. She'd have some tales to tell Molly at the pharmacy, and Penny Saks would want to know everything she had done and seen, and even Ted would probably let her run on about her trip. But it was only New York, not London or Prague or Rome, but if she ever reached the latter, she could at least figure out what to order from the menu.

When the phone rang around seven, she was dressed for the dinner party and thought that perhaps Carolyn Sue or Margaret was checking on her readiness.

To her surprise, it was Gerald Toth.

"Elizabeth, I have just learned from Ted Kelso that he is declining the chance to earn a lot of money by reviewing the ERP. I suppose this was your doing."

"Ted is quite capable of making his own decisions," Betty said. "He suspected almost from the beginning that the program was pirated, and when he knew for certain that it was, he didn't want to be involved with a criminal activity. If you knew Ted at all, you'd see that was the only course he could have taken."

"I understand," Toth said. He sounded tired and sad. "But you did steer people to Brunetta in the matter of Xaviera's murder."

She imagined that those ravishing blue eyes of his were misted by tears at the loss of two loves. "I'm truly sorry for your loss," she said, "and the way it all happened." She didn't want to bring up the fact that he was in part responsible for what had happened with his illegal acquisition of the program. "What will you do now?"

"I expect I'll return the ERP to Beame. Elliott will arrange to do that for money, although it won't be as much as I was going to pay him for getting the program in the first place. And then . . ."

"Seize the years left to you and meet new challenges," Betty said. "That's what I intend to do. You're a young man compared with me. There will be plenty of challenges."

"I think I'll go back to California and sit under my

tree," he said, "and wait for the challenges to march up to me."

"I'm going home myself," Betty said, "in the morning, after I attend a dinner party tonight given by a Mrs. Palliser."

"Gwen invited me," Gerald said, "but I declined, so everyone will have a chance to talk freely about me. I hope we meet again someday, Elizabeth. You're quite a woman."

"Thank you for the compliment," Betty said. "I wish you well."

Now it was time to descend to the lobby to meet Carolyn Sue, but before she could depart, Carolyn Sue was at her door, decked out in silver lamé and the biggest clumps of platinum and diamonds that Betty had ever seen on ears, wrists, neck, and bosom.

"My, don't you look fetchin' tonight. I jus' thought I'd help you move along," Carolyn Sue said. "I want to get Gwen Palliser over as quick as I can. Car's waitin' for us downstairs."

So they were swept away to yet another room filled with painfully slim women and well-barbered men. The hostess had filled another room with many small round tables seating eight and thoughtfully placed Betty and Margaret together at one of them. Carolyn Sue had the place of honor at another table, where a stream of people came and went to greet her and tell her how simply divine she looked after her week at the spa.

The curiosity about Betty's heritage seemed to

have faded a bit, so between bites of salmon she and Margaret were able to talk without fawning interference by the others at the table. Betty even felt reasonably confident that she was not making a spectacle of herself when choosing the one fork out of many for a particular course.

"Elizabeth, I'm planning to go home to Priam's Priory in the spring," Margaret said as a waiter poured red wine for the meat course and took away the white wineglasses emptied during the fish course. "My brother seems to have found himself a bride at last, and of course I want to attend the wedding. I was wondering if you would care to travel with me. I could show you London, and the countryside, and buy you one of those big hats ladies wear to upper-class weddings in England. We could spend some time at Priam's Priory while David is on his honeymoon, and then we might travel to the continent. Oh, forgive me. I shouldn't be arranging your life for you."

"What? Oh, you're not. It sounds lovely." Betty was dazzled by the prospect. "Could we go to Rome perhaps? I've always wanted . . ."

"Of course! I have been intending to visit Paul's father, Prince Aldo, for ages. But he has a reputation for being a ladykiller, so it might be just as well to have a chaperone with me. Now you'll have to be sure your passport is up-to-date."

Betty smiled to herself as Margaret chattered on about things she would need for her European adventure. Her passport was tucked away in the safe at the hotel, along with Gerald's discs. Goodness, she'd have to return them to him before she left. Elliott could fetch them. Nothing was too difficult to overcome.

"Miss Trenka . . ." It was the hostess of the evening, with a very old but distinguished gentleman in tow. "May I present Count Bruno . . ." The rest of his name was lost in a jumble of odd vowel combinations. "He was a friend of your father's." Betty caught Margaret's eye and she winked.

"I think that is not possible," Betty said with aplomb. "He would have mentioned the count, as he was careful to inform his children of the people he believed to be friends. We lived in very difficult times from the war onward. Knowing who our true friends were was important. I do, however, appreciate your taking time to come over to me." She smiled graciously and turned aside as if to dismiss the count.

The count hemmed and spluttered, but Betty ignored him, and soon enough Gwen Palliser led him away.

"Well done," Margaret whispered. "He's a terrible old fraud who likes to pretend that he knows or knew everyone. It's wise not to encourage him."

"It's becoming almost too difficult to deal with all these people," Betty said. "I don't know how you do it, year in and year out."

Margaret frowned. "I don't know how I do it. It's what one does."

Soon enough the dinner ended, the ladies withdrew to sip coffee in a comfortable sitting room, while the men, adhering to fading tradition, stayed behind to smoke their cigars and drink their port.

"Even when I was a girl, my mother abandoned the idea as old-fashioned," Margaret said. "I suppose Gwen thinks it's classy."

The ladies flocked tentatively around Betty, who was determined not to get involved in conversations about her alleged homeland and instead talked about the pleasures of small-town life in Connecticut. As she talked, East Moulton seemed a peaceful paradise compared with life in New York. Carolyn Sue seemed to revel in the chatter and gossip that flowed around her, but she finally seemed to have had enough.

"Even after all that rest at the spa, I'm headin' home," she said. "And I'll be taking Margaret and Miss Trenka away from ya'll, if you don't mind."

Betty didn't mind a bit and was glad to be back at the Villa d'Este, after the car had left Margaret at her home.

Carolyn Sue said, "I was wantin' to ask you if your business with Gerald Toth came off okay. And whether he made a play for Margaret."

"The business went well," Betty said. And then she had to explain about Brunetta and Xaviera, Elliott and Ivor Beame.

"Doesn't that beat all?" Carolyn Sue said. "But

I'm sure glad Sam De Vere didn't get cut out by that blue-eyed charmer."

"I understand that Margaret was with Mr. De Vere last evening," Betty said. "Toth was attentive, but she didn't seem at all interested in him. I think I'll go up and pack now. I'll be leaving before noon. Everyone here at the hotel has been most kind."

"I got me a good staff," Carolyn Sue said. "You sure you don't want a snack or a little glass of wine before retirin'?"

"Heavens, no," Betty said. "In these few days I've eaten and drunk more than I have in any one week in my lifetime."

"You come on down to Dallas for a visit with me, you hear?" And then Carolyn Sue was gone in a blaze of diamonds.

Betty folded her clothes and closed her suitcase. She was feeling like a true jet-setter at the end of a long trip, but the prospect of a visit to England with Margaret and perhaps even Rome made it hard for her to sleep.

Betty arranged to have the discs she'd stored in the hotel safe returned to Gerald Toth. Her personal young man assured her that it would be done at once, and that cut all her ties to Gerald. She departed in the way she had arrived. An ordinary taxi, not a town car, took her to Grand Central Station, and as she waited for the train to New Haven, she stood amid hurrying commuters in the main lobby and examined the blue ceiling and its drawings of the signs of the Zodiac. This time she remembered to buy coffee to take on the train.

By one-thirty she was in New Haven and found Ted waiting outside in his car.

"You look a bit tired," he said.

"It was quite an experience," Betty said, "but I'm glad to be home."

"I have in mind a little detour if you're up to it. Something I thought you might like to see."

She was up to it, and forty-five minutes later they turned off a well-traveled road onto a narrower one lined with trees losing their autumn dress and soon reached the water. Before them was a sparkling expanse of blue tipped by little whitecaps and a long curve of beach. They passed brown-shingled cottages, mostly closed up for the season, many with overturned boats on sawhorses in their driveways.

"This is Redding's Point," Ted said. "That house over there is the one my family rented when I was a kid, and right along here . . ." He pulled into a wide grassy stretch and parked. "Just walk to the top of the steps down to the beach and look to your left. You'll see a pile of rocks at the end of the beach."

He waited in the car while Betty gazed along the beach to the jumble of rocks. She imagined the beautiful Xaviera splashing through the gentle waves that broke on the sand, trailed by the beautiful Brunetta, two girlfriends with common interests in men with money and making good. If she closed her eyes, Betty could see Xaviera climbing over the rocks, the silver disc in her hands, taunting Brunetta to capture it. Then Brunetta pushes her off-balance, grasping her white neck as she reaches for the disc. Xaviera tumbles into the tidal pool, and Brunetta places a foot on her head, forcing her face into the water. The disc slips from Xaviera's grasp and becomes wedged between the rocks.

And the fog rolls in, hiding the sea, the sky, the blond young woman on the pile of wave-worn rocks looking down at her handiwork.

Betty sighed. If that wasn't exactly the way it happened, it was close enough for her. She hoped Sister Rita would approve of the sense of accomplishment she felt for having faced a challenge and overcome it. And this moment at Redding's Point finally brought her adventure to a close.

"I'm ready to go home, Ted," Betty said. "I actually miss my cat."

A CONVERSATION WITH JOYCE CHRISTMAS

Q. *Joyce, you first came to our attention as the creator of socialite sleuth Lady Margaret Priam. But please tell us about Life Before Lady Margaret.*

A. When I graduated from Radcliffe, I didn't plan to be a writer. I wanted to be an editor and book designer. This inspired me to attend the Radcliffe Publishing Procedures course because I thought I would learn a trade and get a job; I didn't want to get an advanced degree and dwell in academia. I did get a job as an editor with a very small Boston publisher, saved my money, and trekked off to Europe to live in Vienna and Rome for a year.

I came back a different person and went to work as an editor at *The Writer* magazine, with the truly legendary Abe and Sylvia Burack, who really did teach me a trade. I got to work with the best writers around, I got to buy carloads of paper (literally tons of it, for the magazine and books), I learned a work ethic that I simply don't see today. And I learned to write letters, an area where the Buracks excelled. Abe died several years ago, but Sylvia carries on, and few are the authors who can resist her letters inviting them to write an article for *The Writer*.

One of my proudest moments was seeing an interview with me in the magazine, later reprinted in the annual *Writer's Handbook*. An even prouder moment was presenting the Raven Award to Sylvia at the 1998 Edgar Awards banquet.

After *The Writer*, I went to live on a tiny Caribbean island for a few years. (I guess I don't stay put easily.) Finally, when I came back to Boston, I noticed that in that big college town, everybody seemed to be a college freshman—but I was not. So I moved to New York, where I freelanced as a copy editor, ghostwriter of a dozen nonfiction books, public relations writer, and advertising copywriter. I have always said, "If they pay me, I will write."

I took a job with a hotel technology consulting firm in New York, not because I know anything about technology, but I am able to write reports about technology that hotel general managers can understand. Now I edit a hotel technology newsletter, write articles for hotel trade magazines, and administer.

Q. *What was your first credit as a published writer?*
A. I believe it was "Three Little Kittens' Christmas," a one-act play for children in *Plays* magazine (another publication of The Writer, Inc.), a work that has been acclaimed as a forerunner to *Cats* and *The Lion King* without the money or the costumes. After ghostwriting nonfiction books, I wrote my first novel, *Hidden Assets*, with a friend, Jon Peterson. He won the coin toss, so it came out under the name Christmas Peterson. Two more unremarkable novels followed under my name, *Blood Child* and *Dark Tide*. Tattered copies of the latter continue to be much beloved in my hometown of Niantic, Connecticut, since it was set there.

Q. *What was your inspiration for the Lady Margaret series?*

A. In an essay I wrote for *Deadly Women*, "The Aristocratic Sleuth," I discussed how I consciously chose to look back to the aristocratic amateur detectives of the Golden Age—Lord Peter Wimsey, Roderick Alleyn, Albert Campion, and so forth—and Lady Margaret was the result.

I happened to be working with just such a titled Englishwoman at a PR firm that promoted society/charity events, so she inspired me to use someone like her for my character. However, she is *not* Lady Margaret, even though her son has been heard to say after reading one of the books, "Mother, did you really do that?" So maybe I got something right about Lady Margaret.

Q. *You're a prolific novelist, but it was one of your short stories, "Takeout," that was nominated for a Macavity Award. How much time do you devote to short fiction?*
A. I don't spend as much time as I'd like. Short stories are a real challenge for me. I think good short story writers have a special gift, and I don't have it, so it's hard work. I write two or so a year, but I'm always thinking about possible tales to tell.

Q. *We know that you devise much of your own publicity and promotion: bookstore readings and autographings, in addition to appearances at libraries, Sisters in Crime events, and the annual Fifth Avenue gala called New York Is Book Country. How important are these promotional appearances?*
A. I think they're very important. They give me a chance to meet readers and potential readers, as well as colleagues. If appearances can help independent mys-

tery bookstores stay in business, they're worth it. Those mystery bookstores are a blessing for us who work in the field.

Q. *Also, each year you're an active participant, as panelist and moderator, at the major crime conferences [Bouchercon, Malice Domestic, the Mid-Atlantic Book Fair and Convention, and others]. Do you have a favorite conference or convention?*
A. I love them all, again because you meet fans and fellow writers. If I have a favorite, it's probably Mid-Atlantic because of its comfortable size and great organization (thanks to Deen Kogan, the founder of Mid-Atlantic). Malice Domestic was my first conference, so it has a special place in my heart. Bouchercon is tremendous and tiring. I also enjoy Cluefest in Dallas, and Landscapes of Mystery at Penn State, a new one that I hope continues, because I am devoted to Penn State football and its ice cream. There are several other reportedly great conferences I haven't had a chance to attend but will do so one day. I especially like conferences where I don't have to get on a plane but can take the train from New York.

The meetings of the International Association of Crime Writers that I've attended in Prague and Vienna have been wonderful. People in Europe tend to be suitably impressed by writers, and it has been very satisfying to get to know writers from other countries.

Q. *You've also served as a national board member of Mystery Writers of America. Was that a good experience? Did you derive any particular insight into the business of crime fiction? Any information/tips you can relay to other writers (or aspiring writers)?*

A. It was Parnell Hall who recruited me to run for the board, but I failed to tell him that I am not particularly good at meetings. Didn't miss one, though. What I learned was that writers expect an organization like MWA to solve all their problems with editors, publishers, agents, bad writing, reduced markets—you name it. Can't be done.

However, the mentor program sponsored by the New York Chapter of MWA assigns published authors to critique the work of new writers. I do it almost every year, including the mentor panel. It is one way I can help aspiring mystery writers. I support Sisters in Crime, too, and had the opportunity to moderate a huge panel at Douglass College [Rutgers] when the Sisters in Crime archives were donated to the Douglass Library, but given my aversion to meetings, I am reluctant to seek office, at least for now.

Tips? My only tip for writers is to read, read, read in the genre you want to write in, then read everything else. And practice, practice, practice writing. Revise, submit it, but don't wait around to hear the good or bad news. Start writing something else immediately. Writers' magazines like *The Writer* are helpful, and a lot of writers say that writers' groups have been valuable for feedback.

Q. *After numerous successful entries in the Lady Margaret Priam series, you devised another series and a new protagonist: retired office manager Betty Trenka, who debuted in* This Business Is Murder. *What was the origin of Betty?*

A. A lot of Betty's background comes from what I do in my day job: running an office. And I'm getting older, although not yet as old as Betty, so dealing with an accumulation of years interests me, always has. In several of the Lady Margaret books, I have older characters, and in my life I've been fortunate to have really close friends who are much older than I.

One example: My first boss was in his seventies and I was a wide-eyed new college graduate when I went to work for him. He finally retired at ninety-nine, but we remained friends until his death. Another dear friend was Hamlin Hunt, who was a well-known writer of short stories for the women's magazines of the 1950s. I think she was the person who gave me the push to become a fiction writer. My aunt Margaret was a feisty old dame masquerading as an elegant, refined Yankee matron. So I was eager to have an older character to write about. Betty's concerns and problems are more like real life than Margaret's, so the change of pace from one series to the other is a pleasure.

Q. *We've heard stories of your daylong fact-finding mission in the food halls of Harrods. Are those stories true? And when you sent Lady Margaret to the Caribbean in* A Perfect Day for Dying, *you surely must have done some on-site research. (How grueling!) What are your most memorable travel and/or research adventures on behalf of Lady Margaret and Betty?*
A. Research is the most fun part of writing. Margaret went to the Caribbean in *A Perfect Day for Dying* because I wanted to write about a place where I lived for a number of years. Of course, I did have to pay a return visit to refresh my memory. As it happens, however, life in the Caribbean is not all fun and sun.

Behind the tourists with bikinis, golf bags, and wet suits is a third world country of poor farmers and fishermen and hardworking women who keep life going and raise their kids to be polite and study hard.

The islands are beautiful, but existence is a struggle, and the wonderful material goods seen on TV are all out of reach. By the way, in my six years there, I think I saw television only once, and knew only one family with a set. I spent a lot of time listening to cricket test matches on the radio, and occasionally joining the little boys in the pick-up cricket games on the beach. I throw like a girl, but they were quite impressed with my batting abilities. All those recess baseball games at Niantic Center Grammar School did me some good after all.

My favorite research adventure took me to Beverly Hills for *A Stunning Way to Die*. Then along the freeway to tour Forest Lawn Cemetery with a native Beverly Hills friend whose parents rest in the mausoleum, and to restaurants owned by my good friend, the late Mauro Vincenti, a genius restaurateur I met years ago in Rome near the Trevi Fountain.

Yes, I did walk the food halls of Harrods for several days to get it right for *Friend or Faux*, and I was taken to an old-fashioned steam circus which figures in the book. Before I wrote *Friend or Faux*, I had the opportunity to visit India, and pulled up that experience to write about the Maharajah and his wives and the country. I try to research everything so I don't make dreadful mistakes, and I use what I've seen and experienced. I'm thinking that Margaret will pay a visit to Rome one of these days, which will require me to pay a return visit.

Q. *Joyce, to conclude, let's offer you the opportunity to play both interviewer and interviewee. Go for it . . .*
A. "Is Christmas your real name?" That's usually Question One. And yes, Christmas is really my name. I was married to someone named Christmas and decided to keep it after the marriage was over. My birth name was Smith, and there are probably already too many mystery writers named Smith. Christmas puts me on the bookshelves next to Agatha Christie, but life in December is one long series of weak attempts at humor. No, I wasn't born on December 25; no, my first name isn't really Merry. You get the idea.

Here's another question: "What do you do in your off (nonworking, nonwriting) hours?" I read a lot of stuff—history, biography, and mysteries. I cook. I keep in touch by e-mail with friends all over the world. I sleep, I wander around New York. Since I have to travel a bit for my job, I get to visit a lot of interesting cities here and abroad. I buy a ton of vintage and modern costume jewelry and, of course, far, far too many books.

If you liked *A Better Class of Murder*,
don't miss any of the Betty Trenka mysteries:

THIS BUSINESS IS MURDER
Betty Trenka's Investigative Debut

DEATH AT FACE VALUE

DOWNSIZED TO DEATH

MOOD TO MURDER